Haydn

Haydn

by J. Cuthbert Hadden

With an Introductory Note by Brian Christensen

Cambridge Scholars Press Ltd.
Adelaide, London, and Washington

Chopin
by J. Cuthbert Hadden (1861-1914), with an introductory note by Brian
Christensen (1966-)
The main body of this book first published in 1902 by J. M. Dent & Co.,
London
The introductory note first published 2002 by

Cambridge Scholars Press

26028 Iverson Drive South Riding, VA 20152 USA
79a Manor Waye, Uxbridge UB8 2BG, UK
21 Desaumarez Street, Kensington Park, South Australia 5068, Australia

British Library Cataloguing in Publication Data
A catalogue record for this book is available from the British Library

A Library of Congress catalogue record for this book has been requested

A National Library of Australia catalogue record for this book has been
requested

ISBN 1904303188

Contents

Introductory Note

Haydn is loved and remembered, most would agree with me, among many other things, for his originality, livelihood, humour, delicacy and measure. But if we were to ask whether these qualities describe Haydn the man or Haydn the composer, most would feel somewhat uncertain as to where one could draw the line. One need not draw a line at all, of course, and claim that with at least certain composers, Haydn among them, there is no major incongruence between man and music. Though one would expect that the conviction behind such a statement is more likely to fade than to be enforced with a thorough reading of a Haydn biography, the reader of Hadden's excellent piece will be left quite satisfied with any neat theory that he may have ventured to construct on the relationship between man and music.

This book brings out the qualities mentioned above with remarkable fervour and persuasion. It is matchlessly amusing to read, and will leave the reader in high spirits, if not considerably enriched by the wealth of information and picturesque sketches or anecdotes. And if the reader is eager for more once he has advanced through the main chapters, he is presented with a selection of Haydn's letters, to allow him to hear the last words from Haydn's own mouth in place of Hadden's. It is worth also mentioning that one is quite likely to encounter a more recent biography executed with greater firmness and furnished with greater accuracy of information, but one will have to look very hard indeed if one wishes to find a more entertaining and amusing account of the great composer's life.

CHAPTER I

BIRTH—ANCESTRY—EARLY YEARS

HAYDN'S position, alike in music and in musical biography, is almost unique. With the doubtful exception of Sebastian Bach, no composer of the first rank ever enjoyed a more tranquil career. Bach was not once outside his native Germany; Haydn left Austria only to make those visits to England which had so important an influence on the later manifestations of his genius. His was a long, sane, sound, and on the whole, fortunate existence. For many years he was poor and obscure, but if he had his time of trial he never experienced a time of failure. With practical wisdom he conquered the Fates and became eminent. A hard, struggling youth merged into an easy middle-age, and late years found him in comfortable circumstances, with a solid reputation as an artist, and a solid retiring-allowance a princely patron, whose house he had served for the better part of his working career. Like Goethe and Wordsworth, he lived out all his life. He was no Marcellus, shown for one brief moment and "withdrawn before his springtime had brought forth the fruits of summer." His great contemporary, Mozart, cut off while yet his light was crescent, is known to posterity only by the products of his early manhood. Haydn's sun set at the end of a long day, crowning his career with a golden splendour whose effulgence still brightens the ever-widening realm of music.

Voltaire once said of Dante that his reputation was becoming greater and greater because no one ever read him. Haydn's reputation is not of that kind. It is true that he may not appeal to what has been called the "fevered modern soul," but there is an old-world charm about him which is specially grateful in our bustling, nerve-destroying, bilious age. He is still known as "Papa Haydn," and the name, to use Carlyle's phrase, is "significant of much." In the history of the art his position is of the first importance. He was the father of instrumental music. He laid the foundations of the modern symphony and sonata, and established the basis of the modern orchestra. Without him, artistically speaking, Beethoven would have been impossible. He seems to us now a figure of a very remote past, so great have been the changes in the world of music since he lived. But his name will always be read in the golden book of classical music; and whatever the evolutionary processes of the art may bring, the time can hardly come when he will be forgotten, his works unheard.

Franz Joseph Haydn was born at the little market-town of Rohrau, near Prugg, on the confines of Austria and Hungary, some two-and-a-half hours' railway journey from Vienna. The Leitha, which flows along the frontier of Lower Austria and Hungary on its way to the Danube, runs near, and the district is flat and marshy. The house in which the composer was born had been built by his father. Situated at the end of the market-place, it was in frequent danger from inundation; and although it stood in Haydn's time with nothing worse befalling it than a flooding now and again, it has twice since been swept away, first in 1813, fours years after Haydn's death, and again in 1833.

It was carefully rebuilt on each occasion, and still stands for the curious to see—a low-roofed cottage, very much as it was when the composer of "The Creation" first began to be "that various thing called man." A fire unhappily did some damage to the building in 1899. But excepting that the picturesque thatched roof has given place to a covering of less inflammable material, the "Zum Haydn" presents its extensive frontage to the road, just as it did of yore. Our illustration shows it exactly as it is to-day.[1] Schindler relates that when Beethoven, shortly before his death, was shown a print of the cottage, sent to him by Diabelli, he remarked: "Strange that so great a man should have been born in so poor a home!" Beethoven's relations with Haydn, as we shall see later on, were at one time somewhat strained; but the years had softened his asperity, and this indirect tribute to his brother composer may readily be accepted as a set-off to some things that the biographer of the greater genius would willingly forget. It was indeed a poor home into which Haydn had been born; but tenderness, piety, thrift and orderliness were there, and probably the happiest part of his career was that which he spent in the tiny, dim-lighted rooms within sound of Leitha's waters.

In later life, when his name had been inscribed on the roll of fame, he looked back to the cottage at Rohrau, "sweet though strange years," with a kind of mingled pride and pathetic regret. Flattered by the great and acclaimed by the devotees of his art, he never felt ashamed of his lowly origin. On the contrary, he boasted of it. He was proud, as he said, of having "made something out of nothing." He does not seem to have been often at Rohrau after he was launched into the world, a stripling not yet in his teens. But he retained a fond memory of his birthplace. When in 1795 he was invited to inspect a monument erected to his honour in the grounds of Castle Rohrau, he knelt down on the threshold of the old home by the marketplace and kissed the ground his feet had trod in the far-away days of youth. When he came to make his will, his thoughts went back to Rohrau, and one of his bequests provided for two of its poorest orphans.

Modern theories of heredity and the origin of genius find but scanty illustration in the case of Haydn. Unlike the ancestors of Bach and Beethoven and Mozart, his family, so far as the pedigrees show, had as little of genius, musical or other, in their composition, as the families of Shakespeare and Cervantes. In the male line they were hard working, honest tradesmen, totally undistinguished even in their sober walk in life. They came originally from Hainburg, where Haydn's great-grandfather, Kaspar, had been among the few to escape massacre when the town was stormed by the Turks in July 1683. The composer's father, Matthias Haydn, was, like most of his brothers, a wheelwright, combining with his trade the office of parish sexton. He belonged to the better peasant class, and, though ignorant as we should now regard him, was yet not without a tincture of artistic taste. He had been to Frankfort during his "travelling years," and had there picked up some little information of a miscellaneous kind. "He was a great lover of music by nature," says his famous son, "and played the harp without knowing a note of music." He had a fine tenor voice, and when the day's toil was over he would gather his household around him and set them singing to his well meant accompaniment.

It is rather a pretty picture that the imagination here conjures up, but it does not help us very much in trying to account for the musical genius of the composer. Even the popular idea that genius is derived from the mother does not hold in Haydn's case. If Frau Haydn had a genius for anything it was merely for moral excellence and religion and the good management of her household. Like Leigh Hunt's mother, however, she was "fond of music, and a gentle singer in her way;" and more than one intimate of Haydn in his old age declared that he still knew by heart all the simple airs which she had been wont to lilt about the house.

The maiden name of this estimable woman was Marie Koller. She was a daughter of the Marktrichter (market judge), and had been a cook in the family of Count Harrach, one of the local magnates. Eight years younger than her husband, she was just twenty-one at her marriage, and bore him twelve children. Haydn's regard for her was deep and sincere;

and it was one of the tricks of destiny that she was not spared to witness more of his rising fame, being cut off in 1754, when she was only forty-six. Matthias Haydn promptly married again, and had a second family of five children, all of whom died in infancy. The stepmother survived her husband—who died, as the result of an accident, in 1763—and then she too entered a second time into the wedded state. Haydn can never have been very intimate with her, and he appears to have lost sight of her entirely in her later years. But he bequeathed a small sum to her in his will, "to be transferred to her children should she be no longer alive."

Joseph Haydn, to give the composer the name which he now usually bears, was the second of the twelve children born to the Rohrau wheelwright. The exact date of his birth is uncertain, but it was either the 3ist of March or the 1st of April 1732. Haydn himself gave the latter as the correct date, alleging that his brother Michael had fixed upon the previous day to save him from being called an April fool! Probably we shall not be far off the mark if we assume with Pohl that Haydn was born in the night between the 3ist of March and the 1st of April.

Very few details have come down to us in regard to his earlier years; and such details as we have refer almost wholly to his musical precocity. It was not such a precocity as that of Mozart, who was playing minuets at the age of four, and writing concertos when he was five; but just on that account it is all the more credible. One's sympathies are with the frank Philistine who pooh-poohs the tales told of baby composers, and hints that they must have been a trial to their friends. Precocious they no doubt were, but precocity often evaporates before it can become genius, leaving a sediment of disappointed hopes and vain ambitions.

In literature, as Mr Andrew Lang has well observed, genius may show itself chiefly in acquisition, as in Sir Walter Scott, who, as a boy, was packing all sorts of lore into a singularly capacious mind, while doing next to nothing that was noticeable. In music it is different. Various learning is not so important as a keenly sensitive organism. The principal thing is emotion, duly ordered by the intellect, not intellect touched by emotion. Haydn's precocity at any rate was of this sort. It proclaimed itself in a quick impressionableness to sound, a delicately strung ear, and an acute perception of rhythm.

We have seen how the father had his musical evenings with his harp and the voices of wife and children. These informal rehearsals were young Haydn's delight. We hear more particularly of his attempts at music-making by sawing away upon a piece of stick at his father's side, pretending to play the violin like the village schoolmaster under whom he was now learning his rudiments. The parent was hugely pleased at these manifestations of musical talent in his son. He had none of the absurd, old-world ideas of Surgeon Handel as to the degrading character of the divine art, but encouraged the youngster in every possible way. Already he dreamt—what father of a clever boy has not done the same?—that Joseph would in some way or other make the family name famous; and although it is said that like his wife, he had notions of the boy becoming a priest, he took the view that his progress towards holy orders would be helped rather than hindered by the judicious cultivation of his undoubted taste for music.

While these thoughts were passing through his head, the chance visit of a relation practically decided young Haydn's future. His grandmother, being left a widow, had married a journeyman wheelwright, Matthias Seefranz, and one of their children married a school-master, Johann Matthias Frankh. Frankh combined with the post of pedagogue that of choir-regent at Hainburg, the ancestral home of the Haydns, some four leagues from Rohrau. He came occasionally to Rohrau to see his relatives, and one day he surprised Haydn keeping strict time to the family music on his improvised fiddle. Some discussion following about the boy's unmistakable talent, the schoolmaster generously offered to take him to Hainburg that he might learn "the first elements of music and other juvenile acquirements." The father was pleased; the mother, hesitating at first, gave her reluctant approval, and Haydn left the family home never to return, except on a flying visit. This was in 1738, when he was six years of age.

The town of Hainburg lies close to the Danube, and looks very picturesque with its old walls and towers. According to the *Nibelungen Lied,* King Attila once spent a night in the place, and a stone figure of that "scourge of God" forms a feature of the Wiener Thor, a rock rising abruptly from the river, crowned with the ruined Castle of Rottenstein. The town cannot be very different from what it was in Haydn's time, except perhaps that there is now a tobacco manufactory, which gives employment to some 2000 hands.

It is affecting to think of the little fellow of six dragged away from his home and his mother's watchful care to be planted down here among strange surroundings and a strange people. That he was not very happy we might have assumed in any case. But there were, unfortunately, some things to render him more unhappy than he need have been. Frankh's intentions were no doubt excellent, but neither in temper nor in character was he a fit guardian and instructor of youth. He got into trouble with the authorities more than once for neglect of his duties, and had to answer a charge of gambling with loaded dice. As a teacher he was of that stern disciplinarian kind which believes in lashing instruction into the pupil with the "tingling rod." Haydn says he owed him more cuffs than gingerbread.

What he owed to the schoolmaster's wife may be inferred from the fact that she compelled him to wear a wig "for the sake of cleanliness." All his life through Haydn was most particular about his personal appearance, and when quite an old man it pained him greatly to recall the way in which he was neglected by Frau Frankh. "I could not help perceiving," he remarked to Dies, "much to my distress, that I was gradually getting very dirty, and though I thought a good deal of my little person, was not always able to avoid spots of dirt on my clothes, of which I was dreadfully ashamed. In fact, I was a regular little urchin." Perhaps we should not be wrong in surmising that the old man was here reading into his childhood the inhabits and sentiments of his later years. Young boys of his class are not usually deeply concerned about grease spots or dishevelled hair.

At all events, if deplorably neglected in these personal matters, he was really making progress with his art. Under Frankh's tuition he attained to some proficiency on the violin and the harpsichord, and his voice was so improved that, as an early biographer puts it, he was able to "sing at the parish desk in a style which spread his reputation through the canton." Haydn himself, going back upon these days in a letter of 1779, says: "Our Almighty Father (to whom above all I owe the most profound gratitude) had endowed me with so much facility in music that even in my sixth year I was bold enough to sing some masses in the choir." He was bold enough to attempt something vastly more ponderous. A drummer being wanted for a local procession, Haydn undertook to play the part. Unluckily, he was so small of stature that the instrument had to be carried before him on the back of a colleague! That the colleague happened to be a hunchback only made the incident more ludicrous. But Haydn had rather a partiality for the drum—a satisfying instrument, as Mr George Meredith says, because of its rotundity—and, as we shall learn when we come to his visits to London, he could handle the instrument well enough to astonish the members of Salomon's orchestra. According to Pohl, the particular instrument upon which he performed on the occasion of the Hamburg procession is still preserved in the choir of the church there.

Hard as these early years must have been, Haydn recognised in after-life that good had mingled with the ill. His master's harshness had taught him patience and self-reliance. "I shall be grateful to Frankh as long as I live," he said to Griesinger, "for keeping me so hard at work." He always referred to Frankh as "my first instructor," and, like Handel with Zachau, he acknowledged his indebtedness in a practical way by bequeathing to Frankh's daughter, then married, 100 florins and a portrait of her father—a bequest which she missed by dying four years before the composer himself.

Haydn had been two years with Frankh when an important piece of good fortune befell him. At the time of which we are writing the Court Capellmeister at Vienna was George Reutter, an inexhaustible composer of church music, whose works, now completely forgotten, once had a great vogue in all the choirs of the Imperial States.

Even in 1823 Beethoven, who was to write a mass for the Emperor Francis, was recommended to adopt the style of this frilled and periwigged pedant! Reutter's father had been for many years Capellmeister at St Stephen's Cathedral, Vienna, and on his death, in 1738, the son succeeded to the post. He had not been long established in the office when he started on a tour of search for choristers. Arriving at Hainburg, he heard from the local pastor of Haydn's "weak but pleasing voice," and immediately had the young singer before him.

The story of the examination is rather amusing. Reutter gave the little fellow a canon to sing at first sight. The boy went though the thing triumphantly, and the delighted Reutter cried "Bravo!" as he flung a handful of cherries into Haydn's cap. But there was one point on which Reutter was not quite satisfied. "How is it, my little man," he said, "that you cannot shake?" "How can you expect me to shake," replied the *enfant terrible,* "when Herr Frankh himself cannot shake?" The great man was immensely tickled by the ready retort, and, drawing the child towards him, he taught him how to make the vibrations in his throat required to produce the ornament. The boy picked up the trick at once. It was the final decision of his fate. Reutter saw that here was a recruit worth having, and he lost no time in getting the parents' sanction to carry him off to Vienna. In the father's case this was easily managed, but the mother only yielded when it was pointed out that her son's singing in the cathedral choir did not necessarily mean the frustration of her hopes of seeing him made a priest.

Thus, some time in the year 1740, Reutter marched away from Hainburg with the little Joseph, and Hainburg knew the little Joseph no more. Vienna was now to be his home for ten long years of dreary pupilage and genteel starvation. In those days, and for long after, St Stephen's Cathedral was described as "the first church in the empire," and it is still, with its magnificent spire, the most important edifice in Vienna. Erected in 1258 and 1276 on the site of a church dating from 1144, it was not finally completed until 1446. It is in the form of a Latin cross, and is 355 feet long. The roof is covered with coloured tiles, and the rich groined vaulting is borne by eighteen massive pillars, adorned with more than a hundred statuettes. Since 1852 the building has been thoroughly restored, but in all essentials it remains as it was when Haydn sang in it as a choir-boy.

Many interesting details have been printed regarding the Choir School of St Stephen's and its routine in Haydn's time. They have been well summarised by one of his biographers.[2]

The Cantorei was of very ancient foundation. Mention is made of it as early as 1441, and its constitution may be gathered from directions given regarding it about the period 1558-1571. It was newly constituted in 1663, and many alterations were made then and afterwards, but in Haydn's day it was still practically what it had been for nearly a century before. The school consisted of a cantor (made Capellmeister in 1663), a sub-cantor, two ushers and six scholars. They all resided together, and had meals in common; and although ample allowance had originally been made for the board, lodging and clothing of the scholars, the increased cost of living resulted in the boys of Haydn's time being poorly fed and scantily clad. They were instructed in "religion and Latin, together with the ordinary subjects of school education, and in music, the violin, clavier, and singing." The younger scholars were taken in hand by those more advanced. The routine would seem to us now to be somewhat severe. There were two full choral services daily in the cathedral. Special *Te Deums* were constantly sung, and the boys had to take part in the numerous solemn processions of religious brotherhoods through the city, as well as in the services for royal birthdays and other such occasions. During Holy Week the labours of the choir were continuous. Children's processions were very frequent, and Haydn's delight in after years at the performance of the charity children in St Paul's may have been partly owing to the reminiscences of early days which it awakened.

But these details are aside from our main theme. The chapel-house of St Stephen's was now the home of our little Joseph. It ought to have been a happy home of instruction, but it was, alas! a house of suffering. Reutter did not devote even ordinary care to his pupil, and from casual lessons in musical theory he drifted into complete neglect. Haydn afterwards declared that he had never had more than two lessons in composition from Reutter, who was, moreover, harsh and cruel and unfeeling, laughing at his pupil's groping attempts, and chastising him on the slightest pretext. It has been hinted that the Capellmeister was jealous of his young charge—that he was "afraid of finding a rival in the pupil." But this is highly improbable. Haydn had not as yet shown any unusual gifts likely to excite the envy of his superior. There is more probability in the other suggestion that Reutter was piqued at not having been allowed by Haydn's father to perpetuate the boy's fine voice by the ancient method of emasculation. The point, in any case, is not of very much importance. It is sufficient to observe that Reutter's name survives mainly in virtue of the fact that he tempted Haydn to Vienna with the promise of special instruction, and gave him practically nothing of that, but a great deal of ill-usage.

Haydn was supposed to have lessons from two undistinguished professors named Gegenbauer and Finsterbusch. But it all amounted to very little. There was the regular drilling for the church services, to be sure: solfeggi and psalms, psalms and solfeggi—always apt to degenerate, under a pedant, into the dreariest of mechanical routine. How many a sweet-voiced chorister, even in our own days, reaches manhood with a love for music? It needs music in his soul. Haydn's soul withstood the numbing influence of pedantry. He realised that it lay with himself to develop and nurture the powers within his breast of which he was conscious. "The talent was in me," he remarked, "and by dint of hard work I managed to get on." Shortly before his death, when he happened to be in Vienna for some church festival, he had an opportunity of speaking to the choirboys of that time. "I was once a singing boy," he said. "Reutter brought me from Hamburg to Vienna. I was industrious when my companions were at play. I used to take my little clavier under my arm, and go off to practise undisturbed. When I sang a solo, the baker near St Stephen's yonder always gave me a cake as a present. Be good and industrious, and serve God continually."

It is pathetic to think of the boy assiduously scratching innumerable notes on scraps of music paper, striving with yet imperfect knowledge to express himself, and hoping that by some miracle of inspiration something like music might come out of it. "I thought it must be all right if the paper was nice and full," he said. He even went the length of trying to write a mass in sixteen parts—an effort which Reutter rewarded with a shrug and a sneer and the sarcastic suggestion that for the present two parts might be deemed sufficient, and that he had better perfect his copying of music before trying to compose it. But Haydn was not to be snubbed and snuffed out in this way. He appealed to his father for money to buy some theory books. There was not too much money at Rohrau, we may be sure, for the family was always increasing, and petty economies were necessary. But the wheelwright managed to send the boy six florins, and that sum was immediately expended on Fux's *Gradus ad Parnassum* and Mattheson's *Volkommener Capellmeister*—heavy, dry treatises both, which have long since gone to the musical antiquary's top shelf among the dust and the cobwebs. These "dull and verbose dampers to enthusiasm" Haydn made his constant companions, in default of a living instructor, and, like Longfellow's "great men," toiled upwards in the night, while less industrious mortals snored.

Meanwhile his native exuberance and cheerfulness of soul were irrepressible. Several stories are told of the schoolboy escapades he enjoyed with his fellow choristers. One will suffice us here. He used to boast that he had sung with success at Court as well as in St Stephen's. This meant that he had made one of the choir when visits were paid to the Palace of Schönbrunn, where the Empress Maria and her Court resided. On the occasion of one of these visits the palace was in the hands of the builders, and the scaffolding presented the usual temptation to the youngsters. "The empress," to quote Pohl, "had caught them climbing it many a time, but her threats and prohibitions had no effect. One day when Haydn was balancing himself aloft, far above his school-fellows, the empress saw him from the windows, and requested her Hofcompositor to take care that 'that fair-headed blockhead,' the ringleader of them all, got '*einen recenten Schilling*' (slang for 'a good hiding')." The command was only too willingly obeyed by the obsequious Reutter, who by this time had been ennobled, and rejoiced in the addition of "von" to his name. Many years afterwards, when the empress was on a visit to Prince Esterhazy, the "fair-headed blockhead" took the cruel delight of thanking her for this rather questionable mark of Imperial favour!

As a matter of fact, the empress, however she may have thought of Haydn the man, showed herself anything but considerate to Haydn the choir-boy. The future composer's younger brother, Michael, had now arrived in Vienna, and had been admitted to the St Stephen's choir. His voice is said to have been "stronger and of better quality" than Joseph's, which had almost reached the "breaking" stage; and the empress, complaining to Reutter that Joseph "sang like a crow," the complacent choirmaster put Michael in his place. The empress was so pleased with the change that she personally complimented Michael, and made him a present of 24 ducats.

One thing leads to another. Reutter, it is obvious, did not like Haydn, and any opportunity of playing toady to the empress was too good to be lost. Unfortunately Haydn himself provided the opportunity. Having become possessed of a new pair of scissors, he was itching to try their quality. The pig-tail of the chorister sitting before him offered an irresistible attraction; one snip and lo! the plaited hair lay at his feet. Discipline must be maintained; and Reutter sentenced the culprit to be caned on the hand. This was too great an indignity for poor Joseph, by this time a youth of seventeen—old enough, one would have thought, to have forsworn such boyish mischief. He declared that he would rather leave the cathedral service than submit. "You shall certainly leave," retorted the Capellmeister, "but you must be caned first." And so, having received his caning, Haydn was sent adrift on the streets of Vienna, a broken-voiced chorister, without a coin in his pocket, and with only poverty staring him in the face. This was in November 1749.

CHAPTER II

VIENNA—1750-1760

THE Vienna into which Haydn was thus cast, a friendless and forlorn youth of seventeen, was not materially different from the Vienna of to-day. While the composer was still living, one who had made his acquaintance wrote of the city: "Represent to yourself an assemblage of palaces and very neat houses, inhabited by the most opulent families of one of the greatest monarchies in Europe—by the only noblemen to whom that title may still be with justice applied. The women here are attractive; a brilliant complexion adorns an elegant form; the natural but sometimes languishing and tiresome air of the ladies of the north of Germany is mingled with a little coquetry and address, the effect of the presence of a numerous Court . . . In a word, pleasure has taken possession of every heart." This was written when Haydn was old and famous; it might have been written when his name was yet unknown.

Vienna was essentially a city of pleasure—a city inhabited by "a proud and wealthy nobility, a prosperous middle class, and a silent, if not contented, lower class." In 1768, Leopold Mozart, the father of the composer, declared that the Viennese public had no love of anything serious or sensible; "they cannot even understand it, and their theatres furnish, abundant proof that nothing but utter trash, such as dances, burlesques, harlequinades, ghost tricks, and devils' antics will go down with them." There is, no doubt, a touch of exaggeration in all this, but it is sufficiently near the truth to let us understand the kind of attention which the disgraced chorister of St Stephen's was likely to receive from the musical world of Vienna. It was Vienna, we may recall, which dumped Mozart into a pauper's grave, and omitted even to mark the spot.

Young Haydn, then, was wandering, weary and perplexed, through its streets, with threadbare clothes on his back and nothing in his purse. There was absolutely no one to whom he could think of turning. He might, indeed, have taken the road to Rohrau and been sure of a warm welcome from his humble parents there. But there were good reasons why he should not make himself a burden on them; and, moreover, he probably feared that at home he would run some risk of being tempted to abandon his cherished profession. Frau Haydn had not yet given up the hope of seeing her boy made a priest, and though we have no definite information that Haydn himself felt a decided aversion to taking orders, it is evident that he was disinclined to hazard the danger of domestic pressure. He had now finally made up his mind that he would be a composer; but he saw clearly enough that, for the present, he must work, and work, too, not for fame, but for bread.

Musing on these things while still parading the streets, tired and hungry, he met one Spangler, a tenor singer of his acquaintance, who earned a pittance at the Church of St Michael. Spangler was a poor man—but it is ever the poor who are most helpful to each other—and, taking pity on the dejected outcast, he invited Haydn to share his garret rooms along with his wife and child. It is regrettable that nothing more is known of this good Samaritan—one of those obscure benefactors who go through the world doing little acts of kindness, never perhaps even suspecting how far-reaching will be the results. He must have died before Haydn, otherwise his name would certainly have appeared in his will.

Haydn remained with Spangler in that "ghastly garret" all through the winter of 1749-1750. He has been commiserated on the garret—needlessly, to be sure. Garrets are famous, in literary annals at any rate; and is it not Leigh Hunt who reminds us that the top storey is healthier than the basement? The poor poet in Pope, who lay high in Drury Lane, "lull'd by soft zephyrs through the broken pane," found profit, doubtless, in his "neighbourhood with the stars." However that may be, there, in Spangler's attic, was Haydn enskied, eager for work—work of any kind, so long as it had fellowship with music and brought him the bare means of subsistence.

"Scanning his whole horizon
in quest of what he could clap eyes on,"

he sought any and every means of making money. He tried to get teaching, with what success has not been recorded. He sang in choirs, played at balls and weddings and baptisms, made "arrangements" for anybody who would employ him, and in short drudged very much as Wagner did at the outset of his tempestuous career. He even took part in street serenades by playing the violin. This last was not a very dignified occupation; but it is important to remember that serenading in Vienna was not the lover's business of Italy and Spain, where the singer is accompanied by guitar or mandoline. It was a much more serious entertainment. It dated from the seventeenth century, if we are to trust Praetorius, and consisted of solos and concerted vocal music in various forms, accompanied sometimes by full orchestra and sometimes by wind instruments alone. Great composers occasionally honoured their patrons and friends with the serenade; and composers who hoped to be great found it advantageous as a means of gaining a hearing for their works. It proved of some real service to Haydn later on, but in the meantime it does not appear to have swelled his lean purse. With all his industry he fell into the direst straits now and again, and was more than once driven into wild projects by sheer stress of hunger.

One curious story is told of a journey to Mariazell, in Styria. This picturesquely situated village has been for many years the most frequented shrine in Austria. To-day it is said to be visited by something like 100,000 pilgrims every year. The object of adoration is the miraculous image of the Madonna and Child, twenty inches high, carved in lime-wood, which was presented to the Mother Church of Mariazell in 1157 by a Benedictine priest. Haydn was a devout Catholic, and not improbably knew all about Mariazell and its Madonna. At any rate, he joined a company of pilgrims, and on arrival presented himself to the local choirmaster for admission, showing the official some of his compositions, and telling of his eight years' training at St Stephen's. The choirmaster was not impressed. "I have had enough of lazy rascals from Vienna," said he. "Be off!" But Haydn, after coming so far, was not to be dismissed so unceremoniously. He smuggled himself into the choir, pleaded with the solo singer of the day to be allowed to act as his deputy, and, when this was refused, snatched the music from the singer's hand, and took up the solo at the right moment with such success that "all the choir held their breath to listen." At the close of the service the choirmaster sent for him, and, apologising for his previous rude behaviour, invited him to his house for the day. The invitation extended to a week, and Haydn returned to Vienna with money enough—the result of a subscription among the choir—to serve his immediate needs.

But it would have been strange if, in a musical city like Vienna, a youth of Haydn's gifts had been allowed to starve. Slowly but surely he made his way, and people who could help began to hear of him. The most notable of his benefactors at this time was a worthy tradesman named Buchholz, who made him an unconditional loan of 150 florins. An echo of this unexpected favour is heard long years after in the composer's will, where we read: "To Fräulein Anna Buchholz, 100 florins, inasmuch as in my youth her grandfather lent me 150 florins when I greatly needed them, which, however, I repaid fifty years ago."

One hundred and fifty florins was no great sum assuredly, but at this time it was a small fortune to Haydn. He was able to do a good many things with it. First of all, he took a lodging for himself—another attic! Spangler had been very kind, but he could not give the young musician the privacy needed for study. It chanced that there was a room vacant, "nigh to the gods and the clouds," in the old Michaelerhaus in the Kohlmarkt, and Haydn rented it. It was not a very comfortable room— just big enough to allow the poor composer to turn about. It was dimly lighted. It "contained no stove, and the roof was in such bad repair that the rain and the snow made unceremonious entry and drenched the young artist in his bed. In winter the water in his jug froze so hard during the night that he had to go and draw direct from the well." For neighbours he had successively a journeyman printer, a footman and a cook. These were not likely to respect his desire for quiet, but the mere fact of his having a room all to himself made him oblivious of external annoyances. As he expressed it, he was "too happy to envy the lot of kings." He had his old, worm-eaten spinet, and his health and his good spirits; and although he was still poor and unknown, he was "making himself all the time," like Sir Walter Scott in Liddesdale.

Needless to say, he was composing a great deal. Much of his manuscript was, of course, torn up or consigned to the flames, but one piece of work survived. This was his first Mass in F (No. II in Novello's edition), erroneously dated by some writers 1742. It shows signs of immaturity and inexperience, but when Haydn in his old age came upon the long-forgotten score he was so far from being displeased with it that he rearranged the music, inserting additional wind parts. One biographer sees in this procedure "a striking testimony to the genius of the lad of eighteen." We need not read it in that way. It rather shows a natural human tenderness for his first work, a weakness, some might call it, but even so, more pardonable than the weakness—well illustrated by some later instances —of hunting out early productions and publishing them without a touch of revision.

It was presumably by mere chance that in that same rickety Michaelerhaus there lived at this date not only the future composer of

"The Creation," but the Scribe of the eighteenth century, the poet and opera librettist, Metastasio.

Born in 1698, the son of humble parents, this distinguished writer had, like Haydn, suffered from "the eternal want of pence." A precocious boy, he had improvised verses and recited them on the street, and fame came to him only after long and weary years of waiting. In 1729 he was appointed Court poet to the theatre at Vienna, for which he wrote several of his best pieces, and when he made Haydn's acquaintance his reputation was high throughout the whole of Europe. Naturally, he did not live so near the clouds as Haydn—his rooms were on the third storey—but he heard somehow of the friendless, penniless youth in the attic, and immediately resolved to do what he could to further his interests. This, as events proved, was by no means inconsiderable.

Metastasio had been entrusted with the education of Marianne von Martinez, the daughter of a Spanish gentleman who was Master of the Ceremonies to the Apostolic Nuncio. The young lady required a music-master, and the poet engaged Haydn to teach her the harpsichord, in return for which service he was to receive free board. Fräulein Martinez became something of a musical celebrity. When she was only seventeen she had a mass performed at St Michael's Church, Vienna. She was a favourite of the Empress Maria Theresa, and is extolled by Burney— who speaks of her "marvellous accuracy" in the writing of English—as a singer and a player, almost as highly as Gluck's niece. Her name finds a place in the biographies of Mozart, who, at her musical receptions, used to take part with her in duets of her own composition. Several of her manuscripts are still in the possession of the Gesellschaft der Musikfreunde. Something of her musical distinction ought certainly to be attributed to Haydn, who gave her daily lessons for three years, during which time he was comfortably housed with the family.

It was through Metastasio, too, that he was introduced to Niccolo Porpora, the famous singing-master who taught the great Farinelli, and whose name is sufficiently familiar from its connection with an undertaking set on foot by Handel's enemies in London. Porpora seems at this time to have ruled Vienna as a sort of musical director and privileged censor, to have been, in fact, what Rossini was for many years in Paris. He was giving lessons to the mistress of Correr, the Venetian ambassador—a "rare musical enthusiast"—and he employed Haydn to act as accompanist during the lessons.

We get a curious insight into the social conditions of the musicians of this time in the bearing of Haydn towards Porpora and his pupil. That Haydn should become the instructor of Fräulein Martinez in no way compromised his dignity; nor can any reasonable objection be raised against his filling the post of accompanist to the ambassador's mistress. But what shall be said of his being transported to the ambassador's summer quarters at Mannersdorf, and doing duty there for six ducats a month and his board—at the servants' table? The reverend author of *Music and Morals* answers by reminding us that in those days musicians were not the confidential advisers of kings like Wagner, rich banker's sons like Meyerbeer, private gentlemen like Mendelssohn, and members of the Imperial Parliament like Verdi. They were "poor devils" like Haydn. Porpora was a great man, no doubt, in his own *métier*. But it is surely odd to hear of Haydn acting the part of very humble servant to the singing-master; blackening his boots and trimming his wig, and brushing his coat, and running his errands, and—playing his accompaniments! Let us, however, remember Haydn's position and circumstances. He was a poor man. He had never received any regular tuition such as Handel received from Zachau, Mozart from his father, and Mendelssohn from Zelter. He had to pick up his instruction as he went along; and if he felt constrained to play the lackey to Porpora, it was only with the object of receiving in return something which would help to fit him for his profession. As he naively said, "I improved greatly in singing, composition, and Italian."[3]

In the meantime he was carrying on his private studies with the greatest assiduity. His Fux and his Mattheson had served their turn, and he had now supplemented them by the first six Clavier Sonatas of Philipp Emanuel Bach, the third son of the great composer. The choice may seem curious when we remember that Haydn had at his hand all the music of Handel and Bach, and the masters of the old contrapuntal school. But it was wisely made. The simple, well-balanced form of Emanuel Bach's works "acted as well as a master's guidance upon him, and led him to the first steps in that style of writing which was afterwards one of his greatest glories." The point is admirably put by Sir Hubert Parry. He says, in effect, that what Haydn had to build upon, and what was most congenial to him, through his origin and circumstances, was the popular songs and dances of his native land, which, in the matter of structure, belong to the same order of art as symphonies and sonatas; and how this kind of music could be made on a grander scale was what he wanted to discover. The music of Handel and Bach leaned too much towards the style of the choral music and organ music of the church to serve him as a model. For their art was essentially contrapuntal—the combination of several parts each of equal importance with the rest, each in a sense pursuing its own course. In modern music the essential principle is harmonic: the chords formed by the combination of parts are derived and developed in reference to roots and keys. In national dances few harmonies are used, but they are arranged on the same principles as the harmonies of a sonata or a symphony; and "what had to be found out in order to make grand instrumental works was how to arrange more harmonies with the same effect of unity as is obtained on a small scale in dances and national songs." Haydn, whose music contains many reminiscences of popular folk-song, had in him the instinct for this kind of art; and the study of Philipp Emanuel's works taught him how to direct his energies in the way that was most agreeable to him.

Although much has been written about Emanuel Bach, it is probable that the full extent of his genius remains yet to be recognised. He was the greatest clavier player, teacher and accompanist of his day; a master of form, and the pioneer of a style which was a complete departure from that of his father. Haydn's enthusiasm for him can easily be explained. "I did not leave the clavier till I had mastered all his six sonatas," he says, "and those who know me well must be aware that I owe very much to Emanuel Bach, whose works I understand and have thoroughly studied. Emanuel Bach himself once complimented me on this fact." When Haydn began to make a name Bach hailed him with delight as a disciple, and took occasion to send him word that, "he alone had thoroughly comprehended his works and made a proper use of them."

This is a sufficient answer to the absurd statement which has been made, and is still sometimes repeated, that Bach was jealous of the young composer and abused him to his friends. A writer in the *European Magazine* for October 1784, says that Bach was "amongst the number of professors who wrote against our rising author." He mentions others as doing the same thing, and then continues "The only notice Haydn took of their scurrility and abuse was to publish lessons written in imitation of the several styles of his enemies, in which their peculiarities were so closely copied and their extraneous passages (particularly those of Bach of Hamburg) so inimitably burlesqued, that they all felt the poignancy of his musical wit, confessed its truth, and were silent." Further on we read that the sonatas of Ops. 13 and 14 were "expressly composed in order to ridicule Bach of Hamburg." All this is manifestly a pure invention. Many of the peculiarities of Emanuel Bach's style are certainly to be found in Haydn's works—notes wide apart, pause bars, surprise modulations, etc.—but if every young composer who adopts the tricks of his model is to be charged with caricature, few can hope to escape. The truth is, of course, that every man's style, whether in music or in writing, is a "mingled yarn" of many strands, and it serves no good purpose to unravel it, even if we could. Haydn's chief instrument was the clavier, but in addition to that he diligently practised the violin. It was at this date that he took lessons on the latter instrument from "a celebrated virtuoso." The name is not mentioned, but the general opinion is that Dittersdorf was the instructor. This eminent musician obtained a situation as violinist in the Court Orchestra at Vienna in 1760; and, curiously enough, after many years of professional activity, succeeded Haydn's brother, Michael, as Capellmeister to the Bishop of Groswardein in Hungary. He wrote an incredible amount of music, and his opera, "Doctor and Apotheker," by which he eclipsed Mozart at one time, has survived up to the present. Whether or not he gave Haydn lessons on the violin, it is certain that the pair became intimate friends, and had many happy days and some practical jokes together. One story connected with their names sounds apocryphal, but there is no harm in quoting it. Haydn and Dittersdorf were strolling down a back street when they heard a fiddler scraping away in a little beer cellar. Haydn, entering, inquired, "Whose minuet is that you are playing?" "Haydn's," answered the fiddler. "It's a—bad minuet," replied Haydn, whereupon the enraged player turned upon him and would have broken his head with the fiddle had not Dittersdorf dragged him away.

It seems to have been about this time—the date, in fact, was 1751—that Haydn, still pursuing his serenading practices, directed a performance of a quintet of his own composition under the windows of Felix Kurz, a well-known Viennese comedian and theatrical manager. According to an old writer, Kurz amused the public by his puns, and drew crowds to his theatre by his originality and by good opera-buffas. He had, moreover, a handsome wife, and "this was an additional reason for our nocturnal adventurers to go and perform their serenades under the harlequin's windows." The comedian was naturally flattered by Haydn's attention. He heard the music, and, liking it, called the composer into the house to show his skill on the clavier. Kurz appears to have been an admirer of what we would call "programme" music. At all events he demanded that Haydn should give him a musical representation of a storm at sea. Unfortunately, Haydn had never set eyes on the "mighty monster," and was hard put to it to describe what he knew nothing about. He made several attempts to satisfy Kurz, but without success. At last, out of all patience, he extended his hands to the two ends of the harpsichord, and, bringing them rapidly together, exclaimed, as he rose from the instrument, "The devil take the tempest." "That's it! That's it!" cried the harlequin, spring-ing upon his neck and almost suffocating him. Haydn used to say that when he crossed the Straits of Dover in bad weather, many years after-wards, he often smiled to himself as he thought of the juvenile trick which so delighted the Viennese comedian.

But the comedian wanted more from Haydn than a tempest on the keyboard. He had written the libretto of an opera, "Der Neue Krumme Teufel," and desired that Haydn should set it to music. The chance was too good to be thrown away, and Haydn proceeded to execute the com-mission with alacrity, not a little stimulated, doubtless, by the promise of 24 ducats for the work. There is a playfulness and buoyancy about much of Haydn's music which seems to suggest that he might have succeeded admirably in comic opera, and it is really to be regretted that while the words of "Der Neue Krumme Teufel" have been preserved, the music has been lost. It would have been interesting to see what the young com-poser had made of a subject which—from Le Sage's "Le Diable Boiteux" onwards—has engaged the attention of so many playwrights and musi-cians. The opera was produced at the Stadt Theatre in the spring of 1752, and was frequently repeated not only in Vienna, but in Berlin, Prague, Saxony and the Breisgau.

An event of this kind must have done something for Haydn's reputa-tion, which was now rapidly extending. Porpora seems also to have been of no small service to him in the way of introducing him to aristocratic acquaintances. At any rate, in 1755, a wealthy musical amateur, the Baron von Fürnberg, who frequently gave concerts at his country house at Weinzierl, near Vienna, invited him to take the direction of these per-formances and compose for their programmes. It was for this nobleman that he wrote his first string quartet, the one in B flat beginning—

This composition was rapidly followed by seventeen other works of the same class, all written between 1755 and 1756.

Haydn's connection with Fürnberg and the success of his compositions for that nobleman at once gave him a distinction among the musicians and *dilettanti* of Vienna. He now felt justified in increasing his
fees, and charged from 2 to 5 florins for a month's lessons. Remembering the legend of his unboylike fastidiousness, and the undoubted natti-
ness of his later years, it is curious to come upon an incident of directly
opposite tendency. A certain Countess von Thun, whose name is associated with Beethoven, Mozart and Gluck, met with one of his clavier
sonatas in manuscript, and expressed a desire to see him. When Haydn
presented himself, the countess was so struck by his shabby appearance
and uncouth manners that it occurred to her he must be an impostor! But
Haydn soon removed her doubts by the pathetic and realistic account
which he gave of his lowly origin and his struggles with poverty, and the
countess ended by becoming his pupil and one of his warmest friends.

Haydn is said to have held for a time the post of organist to the Count
Haugwitz; but his first authenticated fixed engagement dates from 1759,
when, through the influence of Baron Fürnberg, he was appointed
Capellmeister to the Bohemian Count Morzin. This nobleman, whose
country house was at Lukavec, near Pilsen, was a great lover of music,
and maintained a small, well-chosen orchestra of some sixteen or eighteen performers. It was for him that Haydn wrote his first Symphony in D:

We now approach an interesting event in Haydn's career. In the course
of some banter at the house of Rogers, Campbell the poet once remarked
that marriage in nine cases out of ten looks like madness. Haydn's case
was not the tenth. His salary from Count Morzin was only £20 with board
and lodging; he was not making anything substantial by his compositions, and his teaching could not have brought him a large return. Yet,
with the proverbial rashness of his class, he must needs take a wife, and
that, too, in spite of the fact that Count Morzin never kept a married man
in his service! "To my mind," said Mozart, "a bachelor lives only half a
life." It is true enough; but Mozart had little reason to bless the "better
half," while Haydn had less. The lady with whom he originally proposed
to brave the future was one of his own pupils—the younger of the two
daughters of Barber Keller, to whom he had been introduced when he

was a chorister at St Stephen's. According to Dies, Haydn had lodged with the Rollers at one time. The statement is doubtful, but in any case his good stars were not in the ascendant when it was ordained that he should marry into this family.

It was, as we have said, with the younger of the two daughters that he fell in love. Unfortunately, for some unexplained reason, she took the veil, and said good-bye to a wicked world. Like the hero in " Locksley Hall," Haydn may have asked himself, "What is that which I should do?" But Keller soon solved the problem for him. "Barbers are not the most diffident people of the world," as one of the race remarks in "Gil Blas," and Keller was assuredly not diffident. "Never mind," he said to Haydn, "you shall have the other." Haydn very likely did not want the other, but, recognising with Dr Holmes's fashionable lady that "getting married is like jumping overboard anyway you look at it," he resolved to risk it and take Anna Maria Keller for better or worse.

The marriage was solemnised at St Stephen's on November 26, 1760, when the bridegroom was twenty-nine and the bride thirty-two. There does not seem to have been much affection on either side to start with; but Haydn declared that he had really begun to "like" his wife, and would have come to entertain a stronger feeling for her if she had behaved in a reasonable way. It was, however, not in Anna Maria's nature to behave in a reasonable way. The diverting Marville says that the majority of women married to men of genius are so vain of the abilities of their husbands that they are frequently insufferable. Frau Haydn was not a woman of that kind. As Haydn himself sadly remarked, it did not matter to her whether he were a cobbler or an artist. She used his manuscript scores for curling papers and underlays for the pastry, and wrote to him when he was in England for money to buy a "widow's home." He was even driven to pitifully undignified expedients to protect his hard-earned cash from her extravagant hands.

There are not many details of Anna Maria's behaviour, for Haydn was discreetly reticent about his domestic affairs; and only two references can be found in all his published correspondence to the woman who had rendered his life miserable. But these anecdotes tell us enough. For a long time he tried making the best of it; but making the best of it is a poor affair when it comes to a man and woman living together, and the day arrived when the composer realised that to live entirely apart was the only way of ending a union that had proved anything but a foretaste of heaven. Frau Haydn looked to spend her last years in a "widow's home" provided for her by the generosity of her husband, but she predeceased him by nine years, dying at Baden, near Vienna, on the 20th of March 1800. With this simple statement of facts we may finally dismiss a matter that is best left to silence—to where "beyond these voices there is peace."

Whether Count Morzin would have retained the services of Haydn in spite of his marriage is uncertain. The question was not put to the test, for the count fell into financial embarrassments and had to discharge his musical establishment. A short time before this, Prince Paul Anton Esterhazy had heard some of Haydn's compositions when on a visit to Morzin, and, being favourably impressed thereby, he resolved to engage Haydn should an opportunity ever present itself. The opportunity had come, and Haydn entered the service of a family who were practically his life-long patrons, and with whom his name must always be intimately associated.

CHAPTER III

EISENSTADT—1761-1766

As Haydn served the Esterhazys uninterruptedly for the long period of thirty years, a word or two about this distinguished family will not be out of place. At the present time the Esterhazy estates include twenty-nine lordships, with twenty-one castles, sixty market towns, and 414 villages in Hungary, besides lordships in Lower Austria and a county in Bavaria. This alone will give some idea of the power and importance of the house to which Haydn was attached. The family was divided into three main branches, but it is with the Frakno or Forchtenstein line that we are more immediately concerned. Count Paul Esterhazy of Frakno (1635-1713) served in the Austrian army with such distinction as to gain a field-marshal's baton at the age of thirty. He was the first prince of the name, having been ennobled in 1687 for his successes against the Turks and his support of the House of Hapsburg. He was a musical amateur and a performer of some ability, and it was to him that the family owed the existence of the Esterhazy private chapel, with its solo singers, its chorus, and its orchestra. Indeed, it was this prince who, in 1683, built the splendid Palace of Eisenstadt, at the foot of the Leitha mountains, in Hungary, where Haydn was to spend so many and such momentous years.

When Prince Paul died in 1713, he was succeeded by his son, Joseph Anton, who acquired "enormous wealth," and raised the Esterhazy family to "the height of its glory." This nobleman's son, Paul Anton, was the reigning prince when Haydn was called to Eisenstadt in 1761. He was a man of fifty, and had already a brilliant career behind him. Twice in the course of the Seven Years' War he had "equipped and maintained during a whole campaign a complete regiment of hussars for the service of his royal mistress," and, like his distinguished ancestor, he had been elevated to the dignity of field-marshal. He was passionately devoted to the fine arts, more particularly to music, and played the violin with eminent skill. Under his reign the musical establishment at Eisenstadt enjoyed a prosperity unknown at any other period of its history.

As there will be something to say about the terms and nature of Haydn's engagement with Prince Paul Anton, it may be well to quote the text of the agreement which he was required to sign. It was in these terms:

FORM OF AGREEMENT
AND
INSTRUCTIONS FOR THE VICE-CAPELLMEISTER

"This day (according to the date hereto appended) Joseph Heyden *[sic]* native of Rohrau, in Austria, is accepted and appointed Vice-Capellmeister in the service of his Serene Highness, Paul Anton, Prince of the Holy Roman Empire, of Esterhazy and Galantha, etc., with the conditions here following:

1st. Seeing that the Capellmeister at Eisenstadt, by name Gregorius Werner, having devoted many years of true and faithful service to the princely house, is now, on account of his great age and infirmities, unfit to perform the duties incumbent on him, therefore the said Gregorious Werner, in consideration of his long services, shall retain the post of Capellmeister, and the said Joseph Heyden as Vice-Capellmeister shall, as far as regards the music of the choir, be subordinate to the Capellmeister and receive his instructions. But in everything else relating to musical performances, and in all that concerns the orchestra, the Vice-Capellmeister shall have the sole direction.

2nd. The said Joseph Heyden shall be considered and treated as a member of the household. Therefore his Serene Highness is graciously pleased to place confidence in his conducting himself as becomes an honourable official of a princely house. He must be temperate, not showing himself overbearing towards his musicians, but mild and lenient, straightforward and composed. It is especially to be observed that when the orchestra shall be summoned to perform before company, the Vice-Capellmeister and all the musicians shall appear in uniform, and the said Joseph Heyden shall take care that he and all members of his orchestra do follow the instructions given, and appear in white stockings, white linen, powdered, and either with a pig-tail or a tie-wig.

3rd. Seeing that the other musicians are referred for directions to the said Vice-Capellmeister, therefore he should take the more care to conduct himself in an exemplary manner, abstaining from undue familiarity, and from vulgarity in eating, drinking and conversation, not dispensing with the respect due to him, but acting uprightly and influencing his subordinates to preserve such harmony as is becoming in them, remembering how displeasing the consequences of any discord or dispute would be to his Serene Highness.

4th. The said Vice-Capellmeister shall be under an obligation to compose such music as his Serene Highness may command, and neither to communicate such compositions to any other person, nor to allow them to be copied, but to retain them for the absolute use of his Highness, and not to compose anything for any other person without the knowledge and permission of his Highness.

5th. The said Joseph Heyden shall appear in the ante-chamber daily, before and after mid-day, and inquire whether his Highness is pleased to order a performance of the orchestra. After receipt of his orders he shall communicate them to the other musicians and shall take care to be punctual at the appointed time, and to ensure punctuality in his subordinates, making a note of those who arrive late or absent themselves altogether.

6th. Should any quarrel or cause of complaint arise, the Vice-Capellmeister shall endeavour to arrange it, in order that his Serene Highness may not be incommoded with trifling disputes; but should any more serious difficulty occur, which the said Joseph Heyden is unable to set right, his Serene Highness must then be respectfully called upon to decide the matter.

7th. The said Vice-Capellmeister shall take careful charge of all music and musical instruments, and shall be responsible for any injury that may occur to them from carelessness or neglect.

8th. The said Joseph Heyden shall be obliged to instruct the female vocalists, in order that they may not forget in the country what they had been taught with much trouble and expense in Vienna, and, as the said Vice-Capellmeister is proficient on various instruments, he shall take care to practise himself on all that he is acquainted with.

9th. A copy of this agreement and instructions shall be given to the said Vice-Capellmeister and to his subordinates, in order that he may be able to hold them to their obligations therein laid down.

10th. It is considered unnecessary to detail the services required of the said Joseph Heyden more particularly, since his Serene Highness is pleased to hope that he will of his own free will strictly observe not only these regulations, but all others that may from time to time be made by his Highness, and that he will place the orchestra on such a footing, and in such good order, that he may bring honour upon himself, and deserve the further favour of the Prince, his master, who thus confides in his zeal and discretion.

11th. A salary of four hundred florins to be received quarterly is hereby bestowed upon the said Vice-Capellmeister by his Serene Highness.

12th. In addition, the said Joseph Heyden shall have board at the officers' table, or half a gulden a day in lieu thereof.

13th. Finally, this agreement shall hold good for at least three years from May 1st, 1761, with the further condition that if at the conclusion of this term the said Joseph Heyden shall desire to leave the service, he shall notify his intention to his Highness half-a-year beforehand.

14th. His Serene Highness undertakes to keep Joseph Heyden in his service during this time, and should he be satisfied with him, he may look forward to being appointed Capellmeister. This, however, must not be understood to deprive his Serene Highness of the freedom to dismiss the said Joseph Heyden at the expiration of the term, should he see fit to do so.

Duplicate copies of this document shall be executed and exchanged.

Given at Vienna this 1st day of May 1761,

Ad mandatum Celsissimi Principis.

JOHANN STIFFTELL, Secretary."

The situation indicated by this lengthy document has afforded matter for a good deal of comment, and not a little foolish writing. With some it is the old case of Porpora and the blacking of the boots. Thus Miss Townsend remarks: "Our indignation is roused at finding a great artist placed in the position of an upper servant, and required to perform duties almost menial in their nature." That is essentially a modern view. These things have to be judged in relation to the ideas of the age. It was only a few years before this that Johnson had contemptuously thrown away a pair of boots which some pitying soul had placed at the door of his rooms at Pembroke. The British mind likes to think of the sturdy independence of the man who struck the death-blow at patronage in literature. But Johnson himself had the meanest opinion of fiddlers.

There was no talk in Haydn's native country of the dignity of art, at anyrate so far as musicians were concerned. When Mozart first arrived in Vienna in 1781, he had to live with the archbishop's household, and dine at the servants' table. Nay, he was known as "the villain, the low fellow." And is it altogether certain even now, in free Britain, that the parish organist is very clearly distinguished in the squire's mind from the

peripatetic organ-grinder? Public opinion does not seem to have commiserated Haydn on his position of dependence; and, as for Haydn himself, he was no doubt only too glad to have an assured income and a
comfortable home. We may be certain that he did not find the yoke un-
bearably galling. He was of humble birth; of a family which must always
have looked up to their "betters" as unspeakably and immeasurably above
them. Dependence was in the order of nature, and a man of Haydn's
good sense was the last in the world to starve and fret because his freedom to practise his art and develop his powers was complicated with a
sort of feudal service. Some strong souls may find an empty purse the
truest source of inspiration, as Mr Russell Lowell declares it to be; but it
is very much to be doubted whether a careful investigation would show
that a great man's best work was done with the wolf at the door.

Haydn had no self-pity: why should we pity him? He had free quarters
at the palace, with liberty to enjoy the company of his wife when she
chose to favour him—an event of rare occurrence. His salary was raised
from time to time. The old prince, his first employer, paid him 400 florins; his successor increased the amount first to 600 and then to 782 florins (£78); and finally he had 1400 florins, which last sum was continued
to him as a pension when he left the Esterhazy service. Although money
had a much higher purchasing value in those days, the figures here quoted
do not seem princely when we consider the extent and nature of Haydn's
duties, but to a man of Haydn's simple tastes they would appear ample
enough. At least, they would save him from lying on straw and drinking
bad whisky, which Wagner regarded as among the things that are inimi-
cal to the creative genius.

These were the material advantages of the Eisenstadt appointment.
The artistic advantages were even more important, especially to a young
and inexperienced artist who, so far, had not enjoyed many opportunities
of practically testing his own work. Haydn had a very good band always
at his disposal, the members of which were devoted to him. If he wrote
part of a symphony over-night he could try it in the morning, prune,
revise, accept, reject. Many a young composer of to-day would rejoice at
such an opportunity, as indeed Haydn himself rejoiced at it. "I not only
had the encouragement of constant approval," he says, speaking of this
period of his career, "but as conductor of an orchestra I could make
experiments, observe what produced an effect and what weakened it,
and was thus in a position to improve, alter, make additions and omis-
sions, and be as bold as I pleased."

No doubt there were some disadvantages in counterpoise. After the gay life of Vienna, Eisenstadt must have been dull enough, and there is plenty of evidence to show that the young artist occasionally fell into the dumps. In one letter he complains that he "never can obtain leave, even for four-and-twenty hours, to go to Vienna." In another he writes: "I am doomed to stay at home. What I lose by so doing you can well imagine. It is indeed sad always to be a slave, but Providence wills it so. I am a poor creature, plagued perpetually by hard work, and with few hours for recreation." Haydn clearly recognised the necessities of the artist. A quiet life is all very well, but no man ever yet greatly touched the hearts of men if he kept himself too strictly segregated from his kind. Music, like every other art, would perish in a hothouse. Reckon up to-day the composers who are really a force in the emotional life of the people, and ask which of them was reared in the serene, cold air of the academies. A composer to be great must live with his fellows, and open his soul to human affluences.

"I was cut off from the world," says Haydn. "There was no one to confuse or torment me, and I was forced to become original." But his originality was that of an active mind working upon material already stored, and the store had to be replenished in occasional excursions, all too few, from the palace.

The Eisenstadt appointment, then, provided for Haydn's material wants, and gave him opportunities for the peaceful pursuit of his studies, for experiment and self-criticism. He was treated with great consideration by the Esterhazys, and, menial or not, he lived on their bounty and in the friendliest relations with them.

From his agreement with Prince Esterhazy it will have been gathered that, though virtually entrusted with the direction of the Eisenstadt musical establishment, Haydn was really under the control of an old official. Such arrangements seldom work well. The retention of Joseph Werner was presumably due to the thoughtful kindness of his noble patron, but it was bound to lead to awkward situations. Werner had served the Esterhazys for thirty-two years, and could not be expected to placidly accept his supersession by a young and as yet almost unknown musician. True, he was not a very distinguished man himself. He had composed a large amount of music, chiefly sacred, including thirty-nine masses and twelve "Oratorios for Good Friday," besides some grotesque pieces intended as burlesques of the musical life of Vienna. Not one of his works has any real musical value; but, as is usually the case with the talent which stops short of genius, he thought a great deal of himself, and was inclined to look down upon Haydn as an interloper, unskilled in that rigid counterpoint which was the "heaven's law" of the old-time composer. Indeed, he described his associate as "a mere fop" and "a scribbler of songs."

It is but fair to Haydn to say that, if he did not suffer his nominal superior gladly, he at least treated him with respect and a certain deference. He did more. Werner died in 1766, having thus seen only five years of the new order of things, but Haydn's regard for his memory was such that, so late as 1804, he published six of his fugues arranged as string quartets, "out of sincere esteem for this celebrated master." A kindness of heart and a total absence of professional jealousy characterised Haydn throughout his whole career, and never more than in this action.

The composer had been rather less than a twelvemonth in his service when Prince Paul Anton died on the 18th of March 1762. He was succeeded by his brother Nicolaus, a sort of glorified "Grand Duke" of Chandos, who rejoiced in the soubriquet of "The Magnificent." He loved ostentation and glitter above all things, wearing at times a uniform bedecked with diamonds. But he loved music as well. More, he was a performer himself, and played the baryton, a stringed instrument not unlike the viola-da-gamba, in general use up to the end of the eighteenth century. Haydn naturally desired to please his prince, and being perpetually pestered to provide new works for the noble baryton player, he thought it would flatter him if he himself learnt to handle the baryton. This proved an unfortunate misreading of "The Magnificent's" character, for when Haydn at length made his *début* with the instrument, the prince lost no time in letting him understand that he disapproved of such rivalry. An amusing story is told of Kraft, the Eisenstadt cellist, at this time, who occasionally played the second baryton. Kraft presented the prince with a composition into which he had introduced a solo for himself as second baryton. The prince asked to see the part, and proceeded to try it over. Coming to a difficult passage, he exclaimed indignantly: "For the future, write solos only for my part; it is no credit to you to play better than I; it is your duty."

Haydn, so far as we can make out, never essayed the baryton again, but he wrote a surprising amount of music for it, considering its complicated mechanism and the weakness of its tone. In the catalogue of his works there are no fewer than 175 compositions for the instrument—namely, six duets for two barytons, twelve sonatas for baryton and violoncello, twelve *divertimenti* for two barytons and bass, and 125 *divertimenti* for baryton, viola and violoncello; seventeen so-called "cassations"; and three concertos for baryton, with accompaniment of two violins and bass. There is no need to say anything about these compositions, inasmuch as they have gone to oblivion with the instrument which called them into being. At the best they can never have been of much artistic importance.

A new epoch began at Eisenstadt with the rule of Prince Nicolaus. He was a man of unbounded energy himself, and he expected everybody in his service to be energetic too. There is nothing to suggest that Haydn neglected any of his routine duties, which certainly gave him abundant opportunity to "break the legs of time," but once, at least—in 1765—his employer taxed him with lack of diligence in composition, as well as for failing to maintain the necessary discipline among the musicians under his charge. It is likely enough that Haydn was not a rigid disciplinarian; but it must have been a mere whim on the part of Prince Nicolaus to reprove him on the score of laziness in composing. In any case, it seems to have been only a solitary reproof. There is no evidence of its having been repeated, and we may assume that even now it was not regarded as a very serious matter, from the fact that three weeks after the prince was requesting his steward to pay Haydn 12 ducats for three new pieces, with which he was "very much pleased."

Life at Eisenstadt moved on in "calm peace and quiet," but now and again it was stirred into special activity, when Haydn had to put forth his efforts in various new directions. Such an occasion came very early in his service of Prince Nicolaus, when that pompous person made triumphant entry into Eisenstadt. The festivities were on a regal scale and continued for a whole month. A company of foreign players had been engaged to perform on a stage erected in the large conservatory, and Haydn was required to provide them with operettas. He wrote several works of the kind, one of which, "La Marchesa Nepola," survives in the autograph score. Later on, for the marriage of Count Anton, the eldest son of Prince Nicolaus, in 1763, he provided a setting of the story which Handel had already used for his "Acis and Galatea." This work, which was performed by the Eisenstadt *Capelle,* with the orchestra clad in a new uniform of crimson and gold, bore the name of "Acide e Galatea." Portions of the score still exist—a section of the overture, four arias, and a finale quartet. The overture is described as being "in his own style, fresh and cheerful, foreshadowing his symphonies. The songs are in the

Italian manner, very inferior in originality and expression to Handel's music; the quartet is crude in form and uninteresting in substance."[4]

It would seem rather ungracious, as it would certainly be redundant to discuss these "occasional" works in detail. For one thing, the material necessary to enable us to form a correct estimate of Haydn's powers as a dramatic composer is wanting. The original autograph of "Armida," first performed in 1783, is, indeed, preserved. "Orfeo ed Euridice," written for the King's Theatre in the Haymarket in 1791, but never staged, was printed at Leipzig in 1806, and a fair idea of the general style of the work may be obtained from the beautiful air, "Il pensier sta negli oggetti," included in a collection entitled "Gemme d'Antichita." But beyond these and the fragments previously mentioned, there is little left to represent Haydn as a composer of opera, the scores of most of the works written expressly for Prince Esterhazy having been destroyed when the prince's private theatre was burned down in 1779. What Haydn would have done for opera if he had devoted his serious attention to it at any of the larger theatres it is, of course, impossible to say. Judging from what has survived of his work in this department, he was notable for refinement rather than for dramatic power. We must, however, remember the conditions under which he worked. He confessed himself that his operas were fitted only for the small stage at Esterhaz and "could never produce the proper effect elsewhere." If he had written with a large stage in view, it may reasonably be assumed that he would have written somewhat differently.

In 1764 Prince Nicolaus made a journey to Frankfort for the coronation of the Archduke Joseph as King of the Romans. After the festivities connected with that imposing function were over he extended his journey to Paris, where he created some sensation by his extravagant displays of wealth and circumstance. During the Prince's absence Haydn busied himself on a couple of compositions intended to celebrate his home-coming. One was a Te Deum, the other a cantata. The latter work is the more worthy of remark, not because of its music, but because of the fulsomely obsequious manner in which it celebrates the graces and virtues of Nicolaus the Magnificent. The cantata is made up of choruses and duets, a recitative and two arias. Parts of it were afterwards employed in church services. The Te Deum is in C major, and is for four voices with orchestra. It is interesting as an early work, especially if we compare it with the greater Te Deum in the same key composed in the year 1800.

At this point a summary may perhaps be made of the compositions written by Haydn during these five years at Eisenstadt. The list, as given by Pohl, comprises, in addition to the works already named, about thirty symphonies, six string trios, a few *divertimenti* in five parts, a piece for four violins and two 'celli, entitled "Echo," twelve minuets for orchestra, concertos, trios, sonatas and variations for clavier, and, in vocal music, a "Salve Regina" for soprano and alto, two violins and organ. It would serve no useful purpose to deal with these works in detail. The symphonies are, of course, the most important feature in the list, but of these we shall speak generally when treating of Haydn as the father of instrumental music. The first Symphony in C Major, usually called "Le Midi," is of special interest.

The autograph score, dated 1761, and preserved at Eisenstadt, is superscribed, *In Nomine Domini*, and closes with Haydn's customary *Laus Deo* after the final signature. The work is in the usual four movements. The symphonies of this date included also those known in England as "Le Matin" and "Le Soir," the one beginning:

and the other:

Of the string quartets and other instrumental compositions of the period nothing need be said. In all these the composer was simply feeling his way towards a more perfect expression, and as few of them are now performed, their interest for us is almost entirely antiquarian.

CHAPTER IV

ESTERHAZ—1766-1790

To crowd the details of a professional career covering close upon a quarter of a century into a single chapter would, in the case of most of the great composers, be an altogether impossible task. In Haydn's case the difficulty is to find the material for even so slight a record. His life went on smoothly, almost sleepily, as we should now think, in the service of his prince, without personal incident and with next to no disturbance from the outside world. If he had not been a genius of the first rank the outside world would, in all probability, never have heard of his existence.

As it was, his fame was now manifestly spreading. Thus the *Wiener Diarum* for 1766 includes him among the most distinguished musicians of Vienna, and describes him as "the darling of our nation." His amiable disposition, says the panegyrist, "speaks through every one of his works. His music has beauty, purity, and a delicate and noble simplicity which commends it to every hearer. His cassations, quartets and trios may be compared to a pure, clear stream of water, the surface now rippled by a gentle breeze from the south, and anon breaking into agitated billows, but without ever leaving its proper channel and appointed course. His symphonies are full of force and delicate sympathy. In his cantatas he shows himself at once captivating and caressing, and in his minuets he is delightful and full of humour. In short, Haydn is in music what Gellert is in poetry." This comparison with Gellert, who died three years later, was at that date, as Dr Pohl remarks, the most flattering that could well be made. The simplicity and naturalness of Gellert's style were the very antithesis of the pedantries and frigid formalities of the older school; and just as he pioneered the way for the resuscitation of German poetry under Goethe and Schiller, so Haydn may be said to have prepared the path for Beethoven and the modern school. Very likely it was this comparison of the magazine writer that suggested Dittersdorf's remark to Joseph II in 1786, when the emperor requested him to draw an analogy between Haydn's and Mozart's chamber music. Dittersdorf shrewdly replied by asking the emperor in his turn to draw a parallel between Gellert and

Klopstock; whereupon Joseph made answer by saying that both were great poets, but that Klopstock's works required attentive study, while Gellert's beauties were open to the first glance. The analogy, Dittersdof tells us, "pleased the emperor very much." Its point is, however, not very clear—that is to say, it is not very clear whether the emperor meant to compare Klopstock with Haydn and Gellert with Mozart or *vice versa,* and whether, again, he regarded it as more of a merit that the poet and the composer should require study or be "open to the first glance." Joseph was certainly friendly towards Mozart, but by all accounts he had no great love for Haydn, to whose "tricks and nonsense" he made frequent sneering reference.

The first noteworthy event of 1766 was the death of Werner, which took place on March 5. It made no real difference to Haydn, who, as we have seen, had been from the first, in effect, if not in name, chief of the musical establishment; but it at least freed him from sundry petty annoyances, and left him absolutely master of the musical situation. Shortly after Werner's death, the entire musical establishment at Eisenstadt was removed to the prince's new palace of Esterhaz, with which Haydn was now to be connected for practically the whole of his remaining professional career.

A great deal has been written about Esterhaz, but it is not necessary that we should occupy much space with a description of the castle and its surroundings. The palace probably owed its inception to the prince's visit to Paris in 1764. At anyrate, it is in the French Renaissance style, and there is some significance in the fact that a French traveller who saw it about 1782 described it as having no place but Versailles to compare with it for magnificence. The situation—about three and a half miles from Eisenstadt—was anything but suitable for an erection of the kind, being in an unhealthy marsh and "quite out of the world." But Prince Nicolaus had set his heart upon the scheme, as Scott set his heart upon Abbotsford; and just as "Clarty Hole" came in time to be "parked about and gated grandly," so Esterhaz, after something like 11,000,000 gulden had been spent upon it, emerged a veritable Versailles, with groves and grottoes, hermitages and temples, summer-houses and hot-houses, and deer parks and flower gardens. There were two theatres in the grounds: one for operas and dramatic performances generally; the other "brilliantly ornamented and furnished with large artistic marionettes, excellent scenery and appliances."

It is upon the entertainments connected with the latter house that the French traveller just mentioned chiefly dwells. "The prince," he says, "has a puppet theatre which is certainly unique in character. Here the grandest operas are produced. One knows not whether to be amazed or to laugh at seeing 'Alceste,' 'Alcides,' etc., put on the stage with all due solemnity, and played by puppets. His orchestra is one of the best I ever heard, and the great Haydn is his court and theatre composer. He employs a poet for his singular theatre, whose humour and skill in suiting the grandest subjects for the stage, and in parodying the gravest effects, are often exceedingly happy. He often engages a troupe of wandering players for a month at a time, and he himself and his retinue form the entire audience. They are allowed to come on the stage uncombed, drunk, their parts not half learned, and half-dressed. The prince is not for the serious and tragic, and he enjoys it when the players, like Sancho Panza, give loose reins to their humour."

Prince Nicolaus became so much attached to this superb creation of his own, that he seldom cared to leave it. A small portion of the *Capelle* remained at Eisenstadt to carry on the church service there, but the prince seldom went to Eisenstadt, and more seldom still to Vienna. Most of the Hungarian grandees liked nothing better than to display their wealth in the Imperial city during the winter season; but to Haydn's employer there was literally "no place like home." When he did go to Vienna, he would often cut short his visits in the most abrupt manner, to the great confusion of his musicians and other dependants. These eccentricities must have given some annoyance to Haydn, who, notwithstanding his love of quiet and seclusion, often longed for the change and variety of city life. It is said that he was specially anxious to make a tour in Italy about this time, but that ambition had, of necessity, to be abandoned.

There was certainly plenty for him to do at Esterhaz—more than he had ever been required to do at Eisenstadt. Royalties, nobles and aristocrats were constantly at the palace; and music was one of the chief diversions provided for them. The prince was very proud of his musical establishment, and desired to have it considered the best of its kind in Europe. The orchestra of the opera was formed of members of the *Capelle*; "the singers were Italian for the most part, engaged for one, two, or more years, and the books of the words were printed. Numerous strolling companies were engaged for shorter terms; travelling virtuosi often played with the members of the band. Special days and hours were fixed for chamber music, and for orchestral works; and in the interval the singers,

musicians and actors met at the *café,* and formed, so to speak, one family." Something more than creative genius was obviously required to direct the music of an establishment of this kind. A talent for organisation,
an eye for detail, tact in the management of players and singers—these
qualities were all indispensable for the performance of duties such as
Haydn had undertaken. That he possessed them we may fairly assume
from more than one circumstance. In the first place, his employer was
satisfied with him. He raised his salary, listened attentively to all his
suggestions, and did everything that he could to retain his services. In the
second place, his band and singers were sincerely attached to him. They
saw that he had their interests, personal and professional, at heart, and
they "loved him like a father." The prince paid them well, and several of
them were sufficiently capable to receive appointments afterwards in the
Imperial Chapel. Pohl gives a list of the names about this time, but, with
one or two exceptions, they are quite unfamiliar. J. B. Krumpholtz, the
harpist, was engaged from 1773 to 1776, and Andreas Lidl, who played
in London soon after leaving the band, was in the service of the prince
from 1769 to 1774.

The sum paid to Haydn at this date was not large as we should now
consider it, but it was sufficient to free him from financial worry had it
not been for the extravagance and bad management of his wife. The
prince gave him about £78, in addition to which he had certain allow-
ances in kind, and, as we have already said, free quarters for himself and
his wife when she thought fit to stay with him. Probably, too, he was now
making something substantial by his compositions. Griesinger declares
that he had saved about £200 before 1790, the year when he started for
London. If that be true, he must have been very economical. His wife, we
must remember, was making constant calls upon him for money, and in
addition he had to meet the pressing demands of various poor relations.
His correspondence certainly does not tend to show that he was saving,
and we know that when he set out for London he had not only to draw
upon the generosity of his prince for the costs of the journey, but had to
sell his house to provide for his wife until his return.

It is time, however, to speak of some of Haydn's compositions during
this period. At Esterhaz he "wrote nearly al his operas, most of his arias
and songs, the music for the marionette theatre—of which he was particularly fond—and the greater part of his orchestral and chamber works."
The dramatic works bulk rather largely during the earlier part of the period. In 1769, for example, when the whole musical establishment of

Esterhaz visited Vienna, a performance of his opera, "Lo Speciale," was given at the house of Freiherr von Sommerau, and was repeated in the form of a concert. Other works of the kind were performed at intervals, particularly on festival occasions, but as most of them have perished, and all of them are essentially *pièces d'occasion,* it is unnecessary even to recall their names. In 1771 Haydn wrote a "Stabat Mater" and a "Salve Regina," and in 1773 followed the Symphony in C which bears the name of the Empress Maria Theresa, having been written for the empress's visit to Esterhaz in September of that year. In the course of the visit Haydn was naturally introduced to Her Majesty, when, as we have stated, he took occasion to remind her of the "good hiding" she had ordered him to have at Schönbrunn during the old chorister days at St Stephen's. "Well, you see, my dear Haydn," was the reply, "the hiding has borne good fruit."

In 1775 came his first oratorio, "Il Ritorno di Tobia." This is an exceedingly interesting work. It was first performed under Haydn's direction by the Tonkünstler Societät, with solo singers from Esterhaz, at Vienna, on April 2, 1775. In 1784 Haydn added two choruses, one a "Storm Chorus," which is sometimes confused with the "Storm Chorus" (in the same key, but in triple time) composed during his sojourn in London. It is from "Il Ritorno di Tobia" that the so-called motet, "Insanae et Vanae Curae," is adapted, and the "Storm Chorus" immediately follows a fine soprano air in F minor and major, sung by Anna in the original work, a portion of which forms the beautiful second subject (in F) of the "Insanae." The original words of this chorus—"Svanisce in un momento"—are to the effect that the soul threatens to yield to the fury of its enemies, yet trust in God keeps one steadfast. The music admirably reflects these contrasting sentiments, first in the tumultuous D minor section, and then in the tranquillity of the F major portion which follows, no less than in the trustful quietude of the D major conclusion. Latin words were adapted to three of the original choruses, but nothing seems to be known as to the origin of the "Insanae" adaptation. A full score of the motet, published by Breitkopf & Härtel in 1809, was reviewed in the *Allgemeine Musikalische Zeitung* of August 15, 1810, as if it were an entirely original work. The source of the Latin words also remains a mystery. They were presumably put together to fit Haydn's music, but by whom we have no means of ascertaining.

It is interesting to know that Haydn brought the score of his "Il Ritorno di Tobia" with him to England on the occasion of his first visit in 1791, probably with a view to its performance here. Messrs Novello's private library contains an oblong volume in the handwriting of Vincent Novello, in which he has copied some numbers from "Tobia," including the air of Anna already mentioned, but not the "Insanae" chorus. The inside cover of the book bears the following note in Novello's hand, written, not later than 1820, under the contents of the volume: "The whole of the above are unpublished manuscripts, and were copied from an extremely rare volume, containing the full orchestral score of the entire oratorio, kindly lent to me for the purpose by my friend, Mr Shield, who had obtained it from Haydn himself during the visit of the latter to England in the year 1791.—VINCENT NOVELLO, 240 Oxford St."[5] Some of our musical societies in search of novelties might do worse than revive this almost completely-forgotten oratorio. The airs are exceedingly melodious, and the choruses bold and tuneful, with well-developed fugue subjects. The "Insanae" already referred to is frequently performed.

In 1776 Haydn composed "LaVera Costanza" for the Court Theatre of Vienna, but owing to certain intrigues it was declined by the management and produced at Esterhaz instead. The opera was subsequently staged at Vienna in 1790, and six of its airs and a duet were published by Artaria. This incident makes it sufficiently plain that Haydn had his opponents among the musicians and critics of Vienna as well as elsewhere. Burney says a friend in Hamburg wrote him in 1772 that "the genius, fine ideas and fancy of Haydn, Ditters and Filitz were praised, but their mixture of serious and comic was disliked, particularly as there is more of the latter than the former in their works; and as for rules, they knew but little of them." If we substitute "humorous" for "comic," this may be allowed to fully represent the views of the critics and amateurs of Vienna in regard to Haydn's music.

And, unfortunately, the incident just mentioned was not a solitary one. In 1778 Haydn applied for membership to the Tonkünstler Societät, for whom he had in reality written his "Il Ritorno di Tobia." One would have expected such a body to receive him with open arms, but instead of that they exacted a sum of 300 florins on the ground of his non-residence in Vienna! Not only so, but they would fain have brought him under a promise to compose for them whenever they chose to ask him. This latter condition Haydn felt to be impossible in view of his engagement at Esterhaz, and he withdrew his admission fee. That the society were not ashamed of themselves is obvious from a further episode. Some years after this they desired Haydn to rearrange his "Tobia" for a special performance, and when he demanded payment for his trouble they promptly decided to produce Hasse's "Elena" instead. Everything comes to the man who waits. After his second visit to London the Tonkünstler Societät welcomed Haydn at a special meeting, and with one voice appointed him "Assessor Senior" for life. In return for this distinction he presented the society with "The Creation" and "The Seasons," to which gifts, according to Pohl, its prosperity is mainly owing.

If Haydn was thus less highly appreciated at home than he deserved to be, there were others who knew his sterling worth. In 1779 he composed one of his best operas, "L'Isola Disabitata," the libretto of which was by his old benefactor Metastasio, and this work procured his nomination as a member of the Philharmonic Society of Modena. The following extract of a letter written to Artaria in May 1781 is interesting in this connection. He says: "M. le Gros, director of the 'Concerts Spirituels' [in Paris], wrote me a great many fine things about my Stabat Mater, which had been given there four times with great applause; so this gentleman asked permission to have it engraved. They made me an offer to engrave all my future works on very advantageous terms, and are much surprised that my compositions for the voice are so singularly pleasing. I, however, am not in the least surprised, for, as yet, they have heard nothing. If they could only hear my operetta, 'L'Isola Disabitata,' and my last Shrove-tide opera, 'La Fedeltà Premiata,' I do assure you that no such work has hitherto been heard in Paris, nor, perhaps, in Vienna either. My great misfortune is living in the country." It will be seen from this what he thought of "L'Isola," which was not heard in Vienna until its performance at a concert given at the Court Theatre by Willmann the 'cellist in 1785. Haydn sent the score to the King of Spain, who showed his sense of the honour by the gift of a gold snuffbox, set in brilliants. Other marks of royal attention were bestowed upon him about this time. Thus, in 1784, Prince Henry of Prussia sent him a gold medal and his portrait in return for the dedication of six new quartets, while in 1787 King Frederick William II gave him the famous gold ring which he afterwards always wore when composing.

But we have passed somewhat out of our chronological order. The absence of love at home, as we all know, often encourages love abroad. Haydn liked to have an occasional flirtation, as ardent as might be within the bounds of decorum. Sometimes, indeed, according to our insular ideas of such things, he exceeded the bounds of decorum, as in the case of which we are now compelled to speak.

Among the musicians who had been engaged for the Esterhazy service in 1779 were a couple named Polzelli—the husband a violinist, the wife a second-rate vocalist. Luigia Polzelli was a lively Italian girl of nineteen. She does not seem to have been happy with Polzelli, and Haydn's pity was roused for her, much as Shelley's pity was roused for "my unfortunate friend," Harriet Westbrook. The pity, as often happens in such cases, ultimately ripened into a violent passion.

We are not concerned to adopt an apologetic tone towards Haydn. But Signora Polzelli was clearly an unscrupulous woman. She first got her admirer into her power, and then used her position to dun him for money. She had two sons, and the popular belief of the time that Haydn was the father of the younger is perpetuated in several of the biographies. Haydn had certainly a great regard for the boy, made him a pupil of his own, and left him a small sum in his first will, which, however, he revoked in the second. Signora Polzelli's conduct was probably natural enough in the circumstances, but it must have been rather embarrassing to Haydn. After the death of her husband, she wheedled him into signing a paper promising to marry her in the event of his becoming a widower. This promise he subsequently repudiated, but he cared for her well enough to leave her an annuity in his will, notwithstanding that she had married again. She survived him for twenty-three years, and her two daughters were still living at Pesth in 1878.

Returning to 1779, an untoward event of that year was the destruction by fire of the theatre at Esterhaz. The rebuilding of the house was set about at once, the prince having meanwhile gone to Paris, and the reopening took place on October 15, 1780, when Haydn's "La Fedeltà Premiata," already mentioned, was staged. It was about this time that he began to correspond with Artaria, the Vienna music-publisher, with whom he had business dealings for many years. A large number of his letters is given in an English translation by Lady Wallace.[6] They treat principally of business matters, but are not unimportant as fixing the chronological dates of some of his works. They exhibit in a striking way the simple, honest, unassuming nature of the composer; and if they also show him "rather eager after gain, and even particular to a groschen," we must not forget the ever-pressing necessity for economy under which he laboured, and his almost lavish benevolence to straitened relatives and friends. In one letter requesting an advance he writes: " I am unwilling to be in debt to tradesmen, and, thank God! I am free from this burden; but as great people keep me so long waiting for payments, I have got rather into difficulty. This letter, however, will be your security . . . I will pay off the interest with my notes." There is no real ground for charging Haydn with avarice, as some writers have done. "Even philosophers," as he remarked himself, "occasionally stand in need of money;" and, as Beethoven said to George Thomson, when haggling about prices, there is no reason why the "true artist" should not be "honourably paid."

It was about this time too that Haydn opened a correspondence with William Forster of London, who had added to his business of violin-maker that of a music-seller and publisher. Forster entered into an agreement with him for the English copyright of his compositions, and between 1781 and 1787 he published eighty-two symphonies, twenty-four quartets, twenty-four solos, duets and trios, and the "Seven Last Words," of which we have yet to speak. Nothing of the Forster correspondence seems to have survived.

Among the events of 1781-1782 should be noted the entertainments given in connection with two visits which the Emperor Joseph II received from the Grand Duke Paul and his wife. The Grand Duchess was musical, and had just been present at the famous combat between Clementi and Mozart, a suggestion of the Emperor. She had some of Haydn's quartets played at her house and liked them so well that she gave him a diamond snuff-box and took lessons from him. It was to her that he afterwards—in 1802—dedicated his part-songs for three and four voices, while the Grand Duke was honoured by the dedication of the six so-called "Russian" quartets. It had been arranged that the Duke and Duchess should accompany the Emperor to Eisenstadt, but the arrangement fell through, and an opera which Haydn had written for the occasion was only produced at Esterhaz in the autumn of 1782. This was his "Orlando Paladino," better known in its German form as "Ritter Roland." Another work of this year (1782) was the "Mariazell" Mass in C major (Novello, No. 15), which derives its name from the shrine of the Virgin in Styria, the scene of an incident already related. The mass was written to the order of a certain Herr Liebe de Kreutzner, and the composer is said to have taken special pains with it, perhaps because it reminded him of his early struggling days as a chorister in Vienna. It was the eighth mass Haydn had written, one being the long and difficult "Cecilia" Mass in C major, now heard only in a curtailed form. No other work of the kind was composed until 1796, between which year and 1802 the best of his masses were produced. To the year 1783 belongs the opera "Armida," performed in 1784 and again in 1797 at Schickaneder's Theatre in Vienna. Haydn writes to Artaria in March 1784 to say that "Armida" had been given at Esterhaz with "universal applause," adding that "it is thought the best work I have yet written." The autograph score was sent to London to make up, in a manner, for the non-performance of his "Orfeo" there in 1791.

But the most interesting work of this period was the "Seven Words of our Saviour on the Cross," written in 1785. The circumstances attending its composition are best told in Haydn's own words. In Breitkopf & Härtel's edition of 1801, he writes:

> About fifteen years ago I was requested by a Canon of Cadiz to compose instrumental music on the Seven Words of Jesus on the Cross. It was the custom of the Cathedral of Cadiz to produce an oratorio every year during Lent, the effect of the performance being not a little enhanced by the following circumstances. The walls, windows and pillars of the Church were hung with black cloth, and only one large lamp, hanging from the centre of the roof, broke the solemn obscurity. At mid-day the doors were closed and the ceremony began. After a short service the bishop ascended the pulpit, pronounced one of the Seven Words (or sentences) and delivered a discourse thereon. This ended, he left the pulpit and knelt prostrate before the altar. The pause was filled by the music. The bishop then in like manner pronounced the second word, then the third, and so on, the orchestra falling in at the conclusion of each discourse. My composition was to be subject to these conditions, and it was no easy matter to compose seven adagios to last ten minutes each, and follow one after the other without fatiguing the listeners; indeed I found it quite impossible to confine myself within the appointed limits.

This commission may be taken as a further evidence of the growing extent of Haydn's fame. He appears to have been already well known in Spain. Boccherini carried on a friendly correspondence with him from Madrid, and he was actually made the hero of a poem called "The Art of Music," published there in 1779. The "Seven Words" created a profound impression when performed under the circumstances just detailed, but the work was not allowed to remain in its original form, though it was printed in that form by Artaria and by Forster. Haydn divided it into two parts, and added choruses and solos, in which form it was given for the first time at Eisenstadt in October 1797, and published in 1801. The "Seven Words" was a special favourite of the composer himself, who indeed is declared by some to have preferred it to all his other compositions.

The remaining years of the period covered by this chapter being almost totally devoid of incident, we may pause to notice briefly two of the better-known symphonies of the time—the "Toy" Symphony and the more famous "Farewell." The former is a mere *jeu d'esprit,* in which, with an orchestral basis of two violins and a bass, the solo instruments are all of a burlesque character. Mozart attempted something of a kindred nature in his "Musical Joke," where instruments come in at wrong places, execute inappropriate phrases, and play abominably out of tune. This kind of thing does not require serious notice, especially in the case of Haydn, to whom humour in music was a very different matter from the handling of rattles and penny trumpets and toy drums.

The "Farewell" Symphony has often been described, though the circumstances of its origin are generally misstated. It has been asserted, for example, that Haydn intended it as an appeal to the prince against the dismissal of the *Capelle.* But this, as Pohl has conclusively shown, is incorrect The real design of the "Farewell" was to persuade the prince to shorten his stay at *Symphony* Esterhaz, and so enable the musicians to rejoin their wives and families. Fortunately, the prince was quick-witted enough to see the point of the joke. As one after another ceased playing and left the orchestra, until only two violinists remained, he quietly observed, "If all go, we may as well go too." Thus Haydn's object was attained—for the time being! The "Farewell" is perfectly complete as a work of art, but its fitness for ordinary occasions is often minimised by the persistent way in which its original purpose is pointed out to the listener.

Haydn's active career at Esterhaz may be said to have closed with the death, on September 28, 1790, of Prince Nicolaus. The event was of great importance to his future. Had the prince lived, Haydn would doubtless have continued in his service, for he "absolutely adored him." But Prince Anton, who now succeeded, dismissed the whole *Capelle,* retaining only the few members necessary for the carrying on of the church service, and Haydn's occupation was practically gone. The new prince nominally held the right to his services, but there was no reason for his remaining longer at the castle, and he accordingly took up his residence in Vienna. Thus free to employ his time as he considered best, Haydn embraced the opportunity to carry out a long-meditated project, and paid the first of his two visits to London. With these we enter upon a new epoch in the composer's life, and one of great interest to the student and lover of music.

Chapter V,

First London Visit—1791-1792

HAYDN came to England in 1791. It may occur to the reader to ask what England was doing in music at that time, and who were the foremost representatives of the art. The first question may be partially answered from the literature of the period. Thus Jackson, in his *Present State of Music in London*, published the year after Haydn's 1791 arrival, remarks that "instrumental music has been of late carried to such perfection in London by the consummate skill of the performers that any attempt to beat the time would be justly considered as entirely needless." Burney, again, in his last volume, published in 1789, says that the great improvement in taste during the previous twenty years was "as different as civilised people from savages"; while Stafford Smith, writing in 1779, tells that music was then "thought to be in greater perfection than among even the Italians themselves." There is a characteristic John Bull complacency about these statements which is hardly borne out by a study of the lives of the leading contemporary musicians. Even Mr Henry Davey, the applauding historian of English music, has to admit the evanescent character of the larger works which came from the composers of that "bankrupt century." Not one of these composers—not even Arne— is a real personality to us like Handel, or Bach, or Haydn, or Mozart. The great merit of English music was melody, which seems to have been a common gift, but "the only strong feeling was patriotic enthusiasm, and the compositions that survive are almost all short ballads expressing this sentiment or connected with it by their nautical subjects." When Haydn arrived, there was, in short, no native composer of real genius, and our "tardy, apish nation" was ready to welcome with special cordiality an artist whose gifts were of a higher order.

We have spoken of Haydn's visit as a long-meditated project. In 1787 Cramer, the violinist, had offered to engage him on his own terms for the Professional Concerts; and Gallini, the director of the King's Theatre in Drury Lane, pressed him to write an opera for that house. Nothing came of these proposals, mainly because Haydn was too much attached to his prince to think of leaving him, even temporarily. But the time arrived and the man with it. The man was Johann Peter Salomon, a violinist, who, having fallen out with the directors of the professional concerts, had started concerts on his own account. Salomon was a native of Bonn, and had been a member of the Electoral Orchestra there. He had travelled about the Continent a good deal, and no one was better fitted to organise and direct a series of concerts on a large scale. In 1790 he had gone abroad in search of singers, and, hearing of the death of Prince Esterhazy, he set off at once for Vienna, resolved to secure Haydn at any cost. "My name is Salomon," he bluntly announced to the composer, as he was shown into his room one morning. "I have come from London to fetch you; we will settle terms to-morrow."

The question of terms was, we may be sure, important enough for Haydn. But it was not the only question. The "heavy years" were beginning to weigh upon him. He was bordering on threescore, and a long journey in those days was not to be lightly undertaken. Moreover, he was still, nominally at least, the servant of Prince Anton, whose consent, would have to be obtained; and, besides all this, he was engaged on various commissions, notably some for the King of Naples, which were probably a burden on his conscience. His friends, again, do not appear to have been very enthusiastic about the projected visit. There were Dittersdorf and Albrechtsberger, and Dr Leopold von Genzinger, the prince's physician, and Frau von Genzinger, whose tea and coffee he so much appreciated, and who sent him such excellent cream. Above all, there was Mozart—"a man very dear to me," as Haydn himself said.

He had always greatly revered Mozart. Three years before this he wrote: "I only wish I could impress upon every friend of mine, and on great men in particular, the same deep musical sympathy and profound appreciation which I myself feel for Mozart's inimitable music; then nations would vie with each other to possess such a jewel within their frontiers. It enrages me to think that the unparalleled Mozart is not yet engaged at any Imperial Court! Forgive my excitement; I love the man so dearly." The regard was reciprocal. "Oh, Papa," exclaimed Mozart, when he heard of Haydn's intention to travel, "you have had no education for the wide, wide world, and you speak too few languages." It was feelingly said, and Haydn knew it. "My language," he replied, with a smile, "is understood all over the world." Mozart was really concerned at the thought of parting with his brother composer, to whom he stood almost in the relation of a son. When it came to the actual farewell, the tears sprang to his eyes, and he said affectingly: "This is good-bye; we shall never meet again." The words proved prophetic. A year later, Mozart was thrown with a number of paupers into a grave which is now as unknown as the grave of Molière. Haydn deeply lamented his loss; and when his thoughts came to be turned homewards towards the close of his English visit his saddest reflection was that there would be no Mozart to meet him. His wretched wife had tried to poison his mind against his friend by writing that Mozart had been disparaging his genius. "I cannot believe it," he cried; "if it is true, I will forgive him." It was not true, and Haydn never believed it. As late as 1807 he burst into tears when Mozart's name was mentioned, and then, recovering himself, remarked: "Forgive me! I must ever weep at the name of my Mozart."

But to return. Salomon at length carried the day, and everything was arranged for the London visit. Haydn was to have £300 for six symphonies and £200 for the copyright of them; £200 for twenty new compositions to be produced by himself at the same number of concerts; and £200 from a benefit concert. The composer paid his travelling expenses himself, being assisted in that matter by an advance of 450 florins from the prince, which he refunded within the year. In order to provide for his wife during his absence he sold his house at Eisenstadt, the gift of Prince Nicolaus, which had been twice rebuilt after being destroyed by fire.

Salomon sent advance notices of the engagement to London, and on the 30th of December the public were informed through the *Morning Chronicle* that, immediately, on his arrival with his distinguished guest, "Mr Salomon would have the honour of submitting to all lovers of music his programme for a series of subscription concerts, the success of which would depend upon their support and approbation." Before leaving for London Haydn had a tiff with the King of Naples, Ferdinand IV., who was then in Vienna. The composer had taken him some of the works which he had been commissioned to write, and His Majesty, thanking him for the favour, remarked that "We will rehearse them the day after to-morrow." "The day after tomorrow," replied Haydn, "I shall be on my way to England." "What!" exclaimed the King, "and you promised to come to Naples!" With which observation he turned on his heel and indignantly left the room. Before Haydn had time to recover from his astonishment Ferdinand was back with a letter of introduction to Prince Castelcicala, the Neapolitan Ambassador in London; and to show further that the misunderstanding was merely a passing affair he sent the composer later in the day a valuable *tabatière* as a token of esteem and regard.

The journey to London was begun by Haydn and Salomon on the 15th of December 1790, and the travellers arrived at Bonn on Christmas Day. It is supposed, with good reason, that Haydn here met Beethoven, then a youth of twenty, for the first time. Beethoven was a member of the Electoral Chapel, and we know that Haydn, after having one of his masses performed and being complimented by the Elector, the musical brother of Joseph II., entertained the chief musicians at dinner at his lodgings. An amusing description of the regale may be read in Thayer's biography of Beethoven. From Bonn the journey was resumed by way of Brussels to Calais, which was reached in a violent storm and an incessant downpour of rain. "I am very well, thank God!" writes the composer to Frau Genzinger, "although somewhat thinner, owing to fatigue, irregular sleep, and eating and drinking so many different things." Next morning, after attending early mass, he embarked at 7.30, and landed at Dover at five o'clock in the afternoon. It was his first acquaintance with the sea, and, as the weather was rather rough, he makes no little of it in letters written from London. "I remained on deck during the whole passage," he says, "in order to gaze my full at that huge monster—the ocean. So long as there was a calm I had no fears, but when at length a violent wind began to blow, rising every minute, and I saw the boisterous high waves running on, I was seized with a little alarm and a little indisposition likewise." Thus delicately does he allude to a painful episode.

Haydn reached London in the opening days of 1791. He passed his first night at the house of Bland, the music-publisher, at 45 High Holborn, which now, rebuilt, forms part of the First Avenue Hotel. Bland, it should have been mentioned before, had been sent over to Vienna by Salomon to coax Haydn into an engagement in 1787. When he was admitted on that occasion to Haydn's room, he found the composer in the act of shaving, complaining the while of the bluntness of his razor. "I would give my best quartet for a good razor," he exclaimed testily. The hint was enough for Bland, who immediately hurried off to his lodgings and fetched a more serviceable tool. Haydn was as good as his word: he presented Bland with his latest quartet, and the work is still familiarly known as the "Rasirmesser" (razor) Quartet. The incident was, no doubt, recalled when Haydn renewed his acquaintance with the music-publisher.

But Haydn did not remain the guest of Bland. Next day he went to live with Salomon, at 18 Great Pulteney Street, Golden Square, which—also rebuilt—is now the warehouse of Messrs Chatto & Windus, the publishers.[7] He described it in one of his letters as "a neat, comfortable lodging," and extolled the cooking of his Italian landlord, "who gives us four excellent dishes." But his frugal mind was staggered at the charges. "Everything is terribly dear here," he wrote. "We each pay 1 florin 30 kreuzers [about 2S. 8d.] a day, exclusive of wine and beer." This was bad enough. But London made up for it all by the flattering way in which it received the visitor. People of the highest rank called on him; ambassadors left cards; the leading musical societies vied with each other in their zeal to do him honour. Even the poetasters began to twang their lyres in his praise. Thus Burney, who had been for some time in correspondence with him, saluted him with an effusion, of which it will suffice to quote the following lines:

Welcome, great master! to our favoured isle,
Already partial to thy name and style;
Long may thy fountain of invention run
In streams as rapid as it first begun;
While skill for each fantastic whim provides,
And certain science ev'ry current guides!
Oh, may thy days, from human surf' rings free,
Be blest with glory and felicity,
With full fruition, to a distant hour,
Of all thy magic and creative pow'r!
Blest in thyself, with rectitude of mind,
And blessing, with thy talents, all mankind!

Like "the man Sterne" after the publication of *Tristram Shandy*, he was soon deep in social engagements for weeks ahead. "I could dine out every day," he informs his friends in Germany. Shortly after his arrival he was conducted by the Academy of Ancient Music into a "very handsome room" adjoining the Freemasons' Hall, and placed at a table where covers were laid for 200. "It was proposed that I should take a seat near the top, but as it so happened that I had dined out that very day, and ate more than usual, I declined the honour, excusing myself under the pretext of not being very well; but in spite of this, I could not get off drinking the health, in Burgundy, of the harmonious gentlemen present. All responded to it, but at last allowed me to go home." This sort of thing strangely contrasted with the quiet, drowsy life of Esterhaz; and although

Haydn evidently felt flattered by so much attention, he often expressed a wish that he might escape in order to have more peace for work.

His ideas about London were mixed and hesitating. He was chiefly impressed by the size of the city, a fact which the Londoner of to-day can only fully appreciate when he remembers that in Haydn's time Regent Street had not been built and Lisson Grove was a country lane. Mendelssohn described the metropolis as "that smoky nest which is fated to be now and ever my favourite residence." But Haydn's regard was less for the place itself than for the people and the music. The fogs brought him an uncommonly severe attack of rheumatism, which he naively describes as "English," and obliged him to wrap up in flannel from head to foot. The street noises proved a great distraction—almost as much as they proved to Wagner in 1839, when the composer of "Lohengrin" had to contend with an organ-grinder at each end of the street! He exclaimed in particular against "the cries of the common people selling their wares." It was very distracting, no doubt, for, as a cynic has said, one cannot compose operas or write books or paint pictures in the midst of a row. Haydn desired above all things quiet for his work, and so by-and-by, as a solace for the evils which afflicted his ear, he removed himself from Great Pulteney Street to Lisson Grove—"in the country amid lovely scenery, where I live as if I were in a monastery."

For the present the dining and the entertaining went on. The 12th of January found him at the "Crown and Anchor" in the Strand, where the Anacreonatic Society expressed their respect and admiration in the usual fashion.

The 18th of the same month was the Queen's birthday, and Haydn was invited to a Court ball in the evening. This was quite an exceptional distinction, for he had not yet been "presented" at Court. Probably he owed it to the Prince of Wales, afterwards George IV. The Prince was a musical amateur, like his father and his grandfather, whose enthusiasm for Handel it is hardly necessary to recall. He played the cello—"not badly for a Prince," to parody Boccherini's answer to his royal master—and liked to take his part in glees and catches. Haydn was charmed by his affability. "He is the handsomest man on God's earth," wrote the composer. "He has an extraordinary love for music, and a great deal of feeling, but very little money." These courtesies to Haydn may perhaps be allowed to balance the apparent incivility shown to Beethoven and Weber, who sent compositions to the same royal amateur that were never so much as acknowledged.

But even the attentions of princes may become irksome and unprofitable. Haydn soon found that his health and his work were suffering from the flood of social engagements which London poured upon him. The dinner hour at this time was six o'clock. He complained that the hour was too late, and made a resolve to dine at home at four. He wanted his mornings for composition, and if visitors must see him they would have to wait till afternoon. Obviously he was beginning to tire of "the trivial round."

The Salomon concerts should have begun in January, but London, as it happened, was suffering from one of those unreasoning rivalries which made a part of Handel's career so miserable, and helped to immortalise the names of Gluck and Piccini. It is hardly worth reviving the details of such ephemeral contests now. In the present case the factionists were to some extent swayed by financial interests; to a still greater extent by professional jealousies. The trouble seems to have arisen originally in connection with Gallini's preparations for the opening of a new Opera House in the Haymarket. Salomon had engaged Cappelletti and David as his principal vocalists; but these, it appeared, were under contract not to sing in public before the opening of the Opera House. One faction did not want to have the Opera House opened at all. They were interested in the old Pantheon, and contended that a second Italian Opera House was altogether unnecessary.

Salomon's first concert, already postponed to February 25, had been fixed for the 11th of March, on which date David, by special permission, was to appear "whether the Opera house was open or not." The delay was extremely awkward for both Haydn and Salomon, particularly for Haydn. He had been brought to London with beat of drum, and here he was compelled to hide his light while the directors of the professional concerts shot ahead of him and gained the ear of the public before he could assert his superiority. By this time also the element of professional jealousy had come into free play. Depreciatory paragraphs appeared in the public prints "sneering at the composer as 'a nine days' wonder,' whom closer acquaintance would prove to be inferior to either Cramer or Clementi; and alluding to the 'proverbial avarice' of the Germans as tempting so many artists, who met with scanty recognition from their own countrymen to herald their arrival in England with such a flourish of trumpets as should charm the money out of the pockets of easily-gulled John Bull." These pleasantries were continued on rather different lines, when at length Haydn was in a position to justify the claims made for him.

Haydn, meanwhile, had been rehearsing the symphony for his opening concert. Two points are perhaps worth noting here: First, the size and strength of the Salomon Orchestra; and second, the fact that Haydn did not, as every conductor does now, direct his forces, *bâton* in hand. The orchestra numbered between thirty-five and forty performers—a very small company compared with our Handel Festival and Richter Orchestras, but in Haydn's time regarded as quite sufficiently strong. There were sixteen violins, four tenors, three 'celli, four double basses, flutes, oboes, bassoons, trumpets and drums.

Salomon played the first violin and led the orchestra, and Haydn sat at the harpsichord, keeping the band together by an occasional chord or two, as the practice then was. Great composers have not always been great conductors, but Haydn had a winning way with his band, and generally succeeded in getting what he wanted. An interesting anecdote is told by Dies of his first experience with the Salomon Orchestra. The symphony began with three single notes, which the orchestra played much too loudly. Haydn called for less tone a second and a third time, and still was dissatisfied. He was growing impatient. At this point he overheard a German player whisper to a neighbour in his own language: "If the first three notes don't please him, how shall we get through all the rest?" Thereupon, calling for the loan of a violin, he illustrated his meaning to such purpose that the band answered to his requirements in the first attempt. Haydn was naturally at a great disadvantage with an English orchestra by reason of his ignorance of the language. It may be true, as he said, that the language of music "is understood all over the world," but one cannot talk to an orchestra in crotchets and semi-breves.

At length the date of the first concert arrived, and a brilliant audience rewarded the enterprise, completely filling the Hanover Square Rooms, at that time the principal concert hall in London. It had been opened in 1775 by J. C. Bach, the eleventh son of the great Sebastian, when the advertisements announced that "the ladies' tickets are red and the gentlemen's black." It was there that, two years after the date of which we are writing, "Master Hummel, from Vienna," gave his first benefit; Liszt appeared in 1840, when the now familiar term "recital" was first used; Rubinstein made his English *début* in 1842; and in the same year Mendelssohn conducted his Scotch Symphony for the first time in England. In 1844 the "wonderful little Joachim," then a youth of thirteen in a short jacket, made the first of his many subsequent visits to London, and played in the old "Rooms."

So much for the associations of the concert hall in which Haydn directed some of his finest symphonies. And what about the audiences of Haydn's time? It was the day of the Sedan chair, when women waddled in hoops, like that of the lady mentioned in the *Spectator* who appeared "as if she stood in a large drum." Even the royal princesses were, in Pope's phrase, "armed in ribs of steel" so wide that the Court attendants had to assist their ungainly figures through the doorways. Swords were still being worn as a regulation part of full dress, and special weapons were always provided at a grand concert for the use of the instrumental solo performers, who, when about to appear on the platform, were girt for the occasion by an attendant, known as the "sword-bearer."[8]

Haydn's first concert, we have said, was an immense success. Burney records that his appearance in the orchestra "seemed to have an electrical effect on all present, and he never remembered a performance where greater enthusiasm was displayed." A wave of musical excitement appears to have been passing through London, for on this very evening both Covent Garden and Drury Lane Theatres were packed with audiences drawn together by the oratorio performances there. Haydn was vastly pleased at having the slow movement of his symphony encored— an unusual occurrence in those days—and he spoke of it afterwards as worthy of mention in his biography. Fresh from the dinner-table, the audience generally fell asleep during the slow movements! When the novelty of the Salomon concerts had worn off, many of the listeners lapsed into their usual somnolence. Most men in Haydn's position would have resented such inattention by an outburst of temper. Haydn took it good-humouredly, and resolved to have his little joke. He wrote the well-known "Surprise" Symphony. The slow movement of this work opens and proceeds in the most subdued manner, and at the moment when the audience may be imagined to have comfortably settled for their nap a sudden explosive *fortissimo* chord is introduced. "There all the women will scream," said Haydn, with twinkling eyes. A contemporary critic read quite a different "programme" into it. "The 'Surprise,'" he wrote, "might not be inaptly likened to the situation of a beautiful shepherdess who, lulled to slumber by the murmur of a distant waterfall, starts alarmed by the unexpected firing of a fowling-piece." One can fancy the composer's amusement at this highly imaginative interpretation of his harmless bit of waggery.

The same success which attended Haydn's first concert marked the rest of the series. The Prince of Wales's presence at the second concert no doubt gave a certain "lead" to the musical public. We read in one of the newspapers: "It is truly wonderful what sublime and august thoughts this master weaves into his works. Passages often occur which it is impossible to listen to without becoming excited—we are carried away by admiration, and are forced to applaud with hand and mouth. The Frenchmen here cannot restrain their transports in soft adagios; they will clap their hands in loud applause and thus mar the effect."

In the midst of all this enthusiasm the factionists were keeping up their controversy about the opening of Gallini's Theatre. Gallini had already engaged the services of Haydn, together with an orchestra led by Salomon, but nothing could be done without the Lord Chamberlain's licence for the performance of operas. To prevent the issue of that licence was the avowed object of the Pantheon management and their friends. The fight was rendered all the more lively when the Court divided itself between the opposing interests. "The rival theatre," wrote Horace Walpole, "is said to be magnificent and lofty, but it is doubtful whether it will be suffered to come to light; in short the contest will grow political; 'Dieu et mon Droit' (the King) supporting the Pantheon, and 'Ich dien' (the Prince of Wales) countenancing the Haymarket. It is unlucky that the amplest receptacle is to hold the minority."

That was how it turned out. The Lord Chamberlain finally refused his licence for operatic performances, and Gallini had to be content with a licence for "entertainments of music and dancing." He opened his house on the 20th of March, and continued during the season to give mixed entertainments twice a week. Various works of Haydn's were performed at these entertainments, including a cantata composed for David, an Italian catch for seven voices, and the chorus known as "The Storm," a setting of Peter Pindar's "Hark, the wild uproar of the waves." An opera, "Orfeo ed Euridice," to which we have already referred, was almost completed, but its production had necessarily to be abandoned, a circumstance which must have occasioned him considerable regret in view of the store he set upon his dramatic work.

On the 16th of May he had a benefit concert, when the receipts exceeded by £150 the £200 which had been guaranteed. A second benefit was given on May 30, when "La Passione Instrumentale" (the "Seven Words" written for Cadiz) was performed. This work was given again on June 10, at the benefit concert of the "little" Clement, a boy violinist who grew into the famous artist for whom Beethoven wrote his Violin Concerto. On this occasion Haydn conducted for Clement, and it is interesting to observe that Clement took the first violin at the last concert Haydn ever attended, in March 1808.

In the note-book he kept while in London, one of the entries reads: "Anno 1791, the last great concert, with 885 persons, was held in Westminster, Anno 1792, it was transferred to St Margaret's Chapel, with 200 performers. This evoked criticism." Haydn here refers to the Handel Commemoration Festival, the sixth and last of the century. He attended that of 1791, and was much impressed with the grandeur of the performances. A place had been reserved for him near the King's box, and when the "Hallelujah Chorus" was sung, and the whole audience rose to their feet, he wept like a child. "Handel is the master of us all," he sobbed. No one knew the value of Handel's choral work better than Haydn. After listening at the Concert of Antient Music to the chorus, "The Nations tremble," from "Joshua," he told Shield that "he had long been acquainted with music, but never knew half its powers before he heard it, as he was perfectly certain that only one inspired author ever did, or ever would, pen so sublime a composition."[9]

Haydn was no Handel, either as man or artist. Handel declined the Doctor of Music degree with the characteristic remark: "What the devil I throw my money away for that the blockhead wish? "Haydn did not decline it, though probably enough he rated the distinction no higher than Handel did. In the month of July he went down to the Oxford Commemoration, and was then invested with the degree. Handel's latest biographer, Mr W. S. Rockstro, says that the Oxford fees would have cost Handel £100. Haydn's note of the expense is not so alarming: "I had to pay one and a half guineas for the bell peals at Oxforth [sic] when I received the doctor's degree, and half a guinea for the robe." He seems to have found the ceremonies a little trying, and not unlikely he imagined himself cutting rather a ridiculous figure in his gorgeous robe of cherry and cream-coloured silk. At the concert following the investiture he seized the gown, and, raising it in the air, exclaimed in English, "I thank you." "I had to walk about for three days in this guise," he afterwards wrote, "and only wish my Vienna friends could have seen me." Haydn's "exercise" for the degree was the "Canon cancrizans, a tre," set to the words, "Thy voice, O harmony, is divine."

This was subsequently used for the first of the Ten Commandments, the whole of which he set to canons during his stay in London. Three grand concerts formed a feature of the Oxford Commemoration. At the second of these a symphony in G, written in 1787 or 1788, and since known as the "Oxford," was performed, with the composer at the organ. He had taken a new symphony with him for the occasion, but owing to lack of time for rehearsals, the earlier work was substituted. Of this latter, the *Morning Chronicle* wrote that "a more wonderful composition never was heard. The applause given to Haydn was enthusiastic; but the merit of the work, in the opinion of all the musicians present, exceeded all praise."

The London season having now come to an end, Haydn proceeded to recruit his energies by paying visits to distinguished people at their country quarters, taking part in river excursions, picnics, and the like. Prince Esterhazy had sent him a pressing summons to return for a great *fête* which was being organised in honour of the Emperor, but having entered into new engagements with Salomon and others, he found it impossible to comply. A less indulgent employer would have requited him with instant dismissal, but all that the prince said when they afterwards met was, "Ah, Haydn! you might have saved me 40,000 florins." His longest visit at this time was spent with Mr Brassey, a Lombard Street banker, and ancestor of the present peer. "The banker," he says, "once cursed because he enjoyed too much happiness in this world." He gave lessons to Miss Brassey, and "enjoyed the repose of country life in the midst of a family circle all cordially devoted to him." In November he was the guest at two Guildhall banquets—that of the outgoing Lord Mayor on the 5th and that of his successor on the 9th. Of these entertainments he has left a curious account, and as the memorandum is in English it may, perhaps, be reproduced here. It runs as follows in Lady Wallace's translation of the letters:

> I was invited to the Lord Mayor's banquet on November 5. At the first table, No. 1, the new Lord Mayor and his wife dined, the Lord Chancellor, the two sheriffs, the Duke of Lids [Leeds], the minister Pitt, and others of the highest rank in the Cabinet. I was seated at No. 2 with Mr Sylvester, the most celebrated advocate and first King's counsel in London. In this hall, called the Geld Hall [Guildhall], were six tables, besides others in the adjoining room. About twelve hundred persons altogether dined, and everything was in the greatest splendour. The dishes were very nice and well dressed. Wines of every kind in abundance. We sat down to dinner at six o'clock and rose from table at eight. The guests accompanied the Lord Mayor both before and after dinner in their order of precedence.

There were various ceremonies, sword bearing, and a kind of golden crown, all attended by a band of wind instruments. After dinner, the whole of the aristocratic guests of No. 1 withdrew into a private room prepared for them, to have tea and coffee, while the rest of the company were conducted into another room. At nine o'clock No. 1 repaired to a small saloon, when the ball began. There was a raised platform in this room, reserved for the highest nobility, where the Lord Mayor and his wife were seated on a throne. Dancing then commenced in due order of precedence, but only one couple at a time, just as on January 6, the King's birthday. There were raised benches on both sides of this room with four steps, where the fair sex chiefly prevailed. Nothing but minuets were danced in this saloon, but I could only remain for a quarter of an hour, first, because the heat of so many people assembled in such a narrow space was so oppressive, and, secondly, on account of the bad music for dancing, the whole orchestra consisting of two violins and a violoncello; the minuets were more in the Polish style than in our own, or that of the Italians. I proceeded into another room, which really was more like a subterranean cave than anything else; they were dancing English dances, and the music here was a degree better, as a drum was played by one of the violinists![10] I went on to the large hall, where we had dined, and there the orchestra was more numerous, and the music more tolerable. They were also dancing English dances, but only opposite the raised platform where the four first sets had dined with the Lord Mayor. The other tables were all filled afresh with gentlemen, who as usual drank freely the whole night. The strangest thing of all was that one part of the company went on dancing without hearing a single note of the music, or first at one table, and then at another, songs were shouted, or toasts given, amidst the most crazy uproar and clinking of glasses and hurrahs. This hall and all the other rooms were lighted with lamps, of which the effluvia was most disagreeable, especially in the small ball-room. It was remarkable that the Lord Mayor had no need of a carving-knife, as a man in the centre of the table carved everything for him. One man stood before the Lord Mayor and another behind him, shouting out vociferously all the toasts in their order according to etiquette, and after each toast came a flourish of kettledrums and trumpets. No health was more applauded than that of Mr Pitt. There seemed to be no order. The dinner cost £6000, one-half of which is paid by the Lord Mayor, and the other half by the two sheriffs.

In this same month—November—he visited the Marionettes at the Fantoccini Theatre in Saville Row, prompted, no doubt, by old associations with Esterhaz. On the 24th he went to Oatlands to visit the Duke of York, who had just married the Princess of Prussia. "I remained two days," he says, "and enjoyed many marks of graciousness and honour . .

. . On the third day the Duke had me taken twelve miles towards town with his own horses. The Prince of Wales asked for my portrait. For two days we made music for four hours each evening, *i.e.,* from ten o'clock till two hours after midnight. Then we had supper, and at three o'clock went to bed." After this he proceeded to Cambridge to see the university, thence to Sir Patrick Blake's at Langham. Of the Cambridge visit he writes: "Each university has behind it a very roomy and beautiful garden, besides stone bridges, in order to afford passage over the stream which winds past. The King's Chapel is famous for its carving. It is all of stone, but so delicate that nothing more beautiful could have been made of wood. It has already stood for 400 years, and everybody judges its age at about ten years, because of the firmness and peculiar whiteness of the stone. The students bear themselves like those at Oxford, but it is said they have better instructors. There are in all 800 students."

From Langham he went to the house of a Mr Shaw, to find in his hostess the "most beautiful woman I ever saw." Haydn, it may be remarked in passing, was always meeting the "most beautiful woman." At one time she was a Mrs Hodges, another of his London admirers. When quite an old man he still preserved a ribbon which Mrs Shaw had worn during his visit, and on which his name was embroidered in gold.

But other matters now engaged his attention. The directors of the Professional Concerts, desiring to take advantage of his popularity, endeavoured to make him cancel his engagements with Salomon and Gallini. In this they failed. "I will not," said Haydn, "break my word to Gallini and Salomon, nor shall any desire for dirty gain induce me to do them an injury. They have run so great a risk and gone to so much expense on my account that it is only fair they should be the gainers by it." Thus defeated in their object, the Professionals decided to bring over Haydn's own pupil, Ignaz Pleyel, to beat the German on his own ground. It was not easy to upset Haydn's equanimity in an affair of this kind; his gentle nature, coupled with past experiences, enabled him to take it all very calmly. "From my youth upwards," he wrote, "I have been exposed to envy; so it does not surprise me when any attempt is made wholly to crush my poor talents, but the Almighty above is my support . . . There is no doubt that I find many who are envious of me in London also, and I know them almost all. Most of them are Italians. But they can do me no harm, for my credit with this nation has been established far too many years." As a rule, he was forbearing enough with his rivals. At first he wrote of Pleyel: "He behaves himself with great modesty." Later on he remarked that "Pleyel's presumption is everywhere criticised." Nevertheless, "I go to all his concerts, for I love him." It is very pleasant to read all this. But how far Haydn's feelings towards Pleyel were influenced by patriotic considerations it is impossible to say.

The defeated Professionals had a certain advantage by being first in the field in 1792. But Haydn was only a few days behind them with his opening concert, and the success of the entire series was in no way affected by the ridiculous rivalry. Symphonies, *divertimenti* for concerted instruments, string quartets, a clavier trio, airs, a cantata, and other works were all produced at these concerts, and with almost invariable applause. Nor were Haydn's services entirely confined to the Salomon concerts. He conducted for various artists, including Barthelemon, the violinist; Haesler, the pianist; and Madam Mara, of whom he tells that she was hissed at Oxford for not rising during the "Hallelujah" Chorus. The last concert was given on June 6 "by desire," when Haydn's compositions were received with "an ecstasy of admiration." Thus Salomon's season ended, as the *Morning Chronicle* put it, with the greatest *éclat*. Haydn's subsequent movements need not detain us long. He made excursions to Windsor Castle and to Ascot "to see the races," of which he has given an account in his note-book. From Ascot he went to Slough, where he was introduced to Herschel. In this case there was something like real community of tastes, for the astronomer was musical, having once played the oboe, and later on acted as organist, first at Halifax Parish Church, and then at the Octagon Chapel, Bath. The big telescope with which he discovered the planet Uranus in 1781 was an object of great interest to Haydn, who was evidently amazed at the idea of a man sitting out of doors "in the most intense cold for five or six hours at a time."

Visits were also paid to Vauxhall Gardens, where "the music is fairly good" and "coffee and milk cost nothing." "The place and its diversions," adds Haydn, "have no equal in the world." But the most interesting event of this time to Haydn was the meeting of the Charity Children in St Paul's Cathedral, when something like 4000 juveniles took part. "I was more touched," he says in his diary, "by this innocent and reverent music than by any I ever heard in my life!" And then he notes the chant by John Jones: [11]

Curiously enough Berlioz was impressed exactly in the same way when he heard the Charity Children in 1851. He was in London as a juror at the Great Exhibition; and along with his friend, the late G. A. Osborne, he donned a surplice and sang bass in the select choir. He was so moved by the children's singing that he hid his face behind his music and wept. "It was," he says, "the realisation of one part of my dreams, and a proof that the powerful effect of musical masses is still absolutely unknown."[12]

Haydn made many interesting acquaintances during this London visit. Besides those already mentioned, there was Bartolozzi, the famous engraver, to whose wife he dedicated three clavier trios and a sonata in E flat (Op. 78), which, so far unprinted in Germany, is given by Sterndale Bennett in his *Classical Practice*. There was also John Hunter, described by Haydn as "the greatest and most celebrated chyrurgus in London," who vainly tried to persuade him to have a polypus removed from his nose. It was Mrs Hunter who wrote the words for most of his English canzonets, including the charming "My mother bids me bind my hair." And then there was Mrs Billington, the famous singer, whom Michael Kelly describes as "an angel of beauty and the Saint Cecilia of song." There is no more familiar anecdote than that which connects Haydn with Sir Joshua Reynolds's portrait of this notorious character. Carpani is responsible for the tale. He says that Haydn one day found Mrs Billington sitting to Reynolds, who was painting her as St Cecilia listening to the angels. "It is like," said Haydn, "but there is a strange mistake." "What is that?" asked Reynolds. "You have painted her listening to the angels. You ought to have represented the angels listening to her." It is a very pretty story, but it cannot possibly be true. Reynolds's portrait of Mrs Billington was painted in 1789, two years before Haydn's arrival, and was actually shown in the Academy Exhibition of 1790, the last to which Sir Joshua contributed.[13] Of course Haydn may have made the witty remark here attributed to him, but it cannot have been at the time of the painting of the portrait. That he was an enthusiastic admirer of Mrs Billington there can be no doubt.

There was another intimacy of more import, about which it is necessary to speak at some length. When Dies published his biography of Haydn in 1810 he referred to a batch of love-letters written to the composer during this visit to London. The existence of the letters was known to Pohl, who devotes a part of his *Haydn in London* to them, and prints certain extracts; but the letters themselves do not appear to have been printed either in the original English or in a German translation until Mr Henry E. Krehbiel, the well-known American musical critic, gave them to the world through the columns of the New York *Tribune*. Mr Krehbiel was enabled to do this by coming into possession of a transcript of Haydn's London note-book, with which we will deal presently. Haydn, as he informs us, had copied all the letters out in full, "a proceeding which tells its own story touching his feelings towards the missives and their fair author." He preserved them most carefully among the souvenirs of his visit, and when Dies asked him about them, he replied: "They are letters from an English widow in London, who loved me. Though sixty years old, she was still lovely and amiable, and I should in all likelihood have married her if I had been single." Who was the lady thus celebrated? In Haydn's note-book the following entry occurs: "Mistress Schroeter, No. 6 James Street, Buckingham Gate." The inquiry is here answered: Mistress Schroeter was the lady.

Haydn, it will be seen, describes her as a widow of sixty. According to Goldsmith, women and music should never be dated; but in the present case, there is a not unnatural curiosity to discover the lady's age. Mr Krehbiel gives good grounds for doubting Haydn's statement that Mistress Schroeter was sixty when he met her.

She had been married to Johann Samuel Schroeter, an excellent German musician, who settled in London in 1772. Schroeter died in 1788, three years before the date of Haydn's visit, when he was just thirty-eight. Now Dr Burney, who must have known the family, says that Schroeter "married a young lady of considerable fortune, who was his scholar, and was in easy circumstances." If, therefore, Mrs Schroeter was sixty years old when Haydn made her acquaintance, she must have been nineteen years her husband's senior, and could not very well be described as a "young" lady at the time of her marriage.

It is, however, unnecessary to dwell upon the matter of age. The interesting point is that Haydn fell under the spell of the charming widow. There is no account of their first meeting; but it was probably of a purely professional nature. Towards the end of June 1791 the lady writes: "Mrs Schroeter presents her compliments to Mr Haydn, and informs him she is just returned to town, and will be very happy to see him whenever it is convenient to him to give her a lesson." A woman of sixty should hardly have been requiring lessons, especially after having been the wife of a professor who succeeded the "English Bach" as music-master to the Queen. But lessons sometimes cover a good deal of love-making, and that was clearly the case with Haydn and Mrs Schroeter.

There is indeed some reason to doubt if the lessons were continued. At any rate, by February 1792, the affair had ripened so far as to allow the lady to address the composer as "my dear," and disclose her tender solicitude for his health. On the 7th of the following month she writes that she was "extremely sorry" to part with him; so suddenly the previous night. "Our conversation was particularly interesting, and I had a thousand affectionate things to say to you. My heart was and is full of tenderness for you, but no language can express half the love and affection I feel for you. You are dearer to me every day of my life."

This was pretty warm, considering that Haydn was still in the bonds of wedlock. We cannot tell how far he reciprocated the feeling, his letters, if he wrote any, not having been preserved; but it may be safely inferred that a lady who was to be " happy to see you both in the morning and the evening" did not do all the love-making. On the 4th of April the composer gets a present of soap, and is the "ever dear Haydn" of the "invariable and truly affectionate" Mistress Schroeter. He had been working too hard about this particular date (he notes that he was "bled in London" on the 17th of March), and on the 12th the "loveress," to use Marjorie Fleming's term, is "truly anxious" about her "dear love," for whom her regard is "stronger every day." An extract from the letter of April 19 may be quoted as it stands:

> I was extremely sorry to hear this morning that you were indisposed. I am told you were five hours at your studys yesterday. Indeed, my dear love, I am afraid it will hurt you. Why should you, who have already produced so many wonderful and charming compositions, still fatigue yourself with such close application? I almost tremble for your health. Let me prevail on you, my much-loved Haydn, not to keep to your studys so long at one time. My dear love, if you could know how very precious your

welfare is to me, I flatter myself you would endeavour to preserve it for my sake as well as your own.

The next letter shows that Haydn had been deriving some profit from Mistress Schroeter's affections by setting her to work as an amanuensis. She has been copying out a march, and is sorry that she has not done it better. "If my Haydn would employ me oftener to write music, I hope I should improve; and I know I should delight in the occupation." Invitations to dine at St James's Street are repeatedly being sent, for Mistress Schroeter wishes "to have as much of your company as possible." When others are expected, Haydn is to come early, so that they may have some time together "before the rest of our friends come." Does the adored Schroeter go to one of her "dearest love's" concerts, she thanks him a thousand times for the entertainment. "Where your sweet compositions and your excellent performance combine," she writes, "it cannot fail of being the most charming concert; but, apart from that, the pleasure of seeing you must ever give me infinite satisfaction." As the time drew near for Haydn's departure, "every moment of your company is more and more precious to me." She begs to assure him with "heart-felt affection" that she will ever consider the acquaintance with him as one of the chief blessings of her life. Nay, she entertains for her "dearest Haydn," "the fondest and tenderest affection the human heart is capable of." And so on.

One feels almost brutally rude in breaking in upon the privacy of this little romance. No doubt the flirtation was inexcusable enough on certain grounds. But taking the whole circumstances into account—above all, the loveless, childless home of the composer—the biographer is disposed to see in the episode merely that human yearning after affection and sympathy which has been denied to Haydn where he had most right to expect them. He admitted that he was apt to be fascinated by pretty and amiable women, and the woman to whom he had given his name was neither pretty nor amiable. An ancient philosopher has said that a man should never marry a plain woman, since his affections would always be in danger of straying when he met a beauty. This incident in Haydn's career would seem to support the philosopher's contention. For the rest, it was probably harmless enough, for there is nothing to show that the severer codes of morality were infringed.

The biographers of Haydn have not succeeded in discovering how the Schroeter *amourette* ended. The letters printed by Mr Krehbiel are all confined to the year 1792, and mention is nowhere made of any of later date. When Haydn returned to London in 1794, he occupied rooms at No. 1 Bury Street, St James', and Pohl suggests that he may have owed the more pleasant quarters to his old admirer, who would naturally be anxious to have him as near her as possible. A short walk of ten minutes through St James' Park and the Mall would bring him to Buckingham Palace, and from that to Mrs Schroeter's was only a stone-throw. Whether the old affectionate relations were resumed it is impossible to say. If there were any letters of the second London visit, it is curious that Haydn should not have preserved them with the rest. There is no ground for supposing that any disagreement came between the pair: the facts point rather the other way. When Haydn finally said farewell to London, he left the scores of his six last symphonies "in the hands of a lady." Pohl thinks the lady was Mrs Schroeter, and doubtless he is right. At any rate Haydn's esteem for her, to use no stronger term, is sufficiently empha-sised by his having inscribed to her the three trios numbered 1, 2 and 6 in the Breitkopf & Härtel list.

Reference has already been made to the diary or notebook kept by Haydn during his visit. The original manuscript of this curious document came into the hands of his friend, Joseph Weigl, whose father had been 'cellist to Prince Esterhazy. A similar diary was kept during the second visit, but this was lost; and indeed the first note-book narrowly escaped destruction at the hands of a careless domestic. Haydn's autograph was at one time in the possession of Dr Pohl. A copy of it made by A. W. Thayer, the biographer of Beethoven, in 1862, became, as previously stated, the property of Mr Krehbiel, who has printed the entries, with running comment, in his *Music and Manners in the Classical Period* (London, 1898). Mr Krehbiel rightly describes some of the entries as mere "vague mnemonic hints," and adds that one entry which descants in epigrammatic fashion on the comparative morals of the women of France, Holland and England is unfit for publication. Looking over the diary, it is instructive to observe how little reference is made to music. One or two of the entries are plainly memoranda of purchases to be made for friends. There is one note about the National Debt of England, another about the trial of Warren Hastings. London, we learn, has 4000 carts for cleaning the streets, and consumes annually 800,000 cartloads of coals. That scandalous book, the *Memoirs of Mrs Billington,* which had just been published, forms the subject of a long entry. "It is said that her [Mrs Billington's] character is very faulty, but nevertheless she is a great genius, and all the women hate her because she is so beautiful." A note is made of the constituents of the Prince of Wales's punch—"One bottle champagne, one bottle Burgundy, one bottle rum, ten lemons, two oranges, pound and a half of sugar." A process for preserving milk "for a long time " is also described. We read that on the 5th of November (1791) "there was a fog so thick that one might have spread it on bread. In order to write I had to light a candle as early as eleven o'clock." Here is a curious item—"In the month of June 1792 a chicken, 7s.; an Indian [a kind of bittern found in North America] 9s.; a dozen larks, 1 coron [? crown]. *N.B.*—If plucked, a duck, 5s."

Haydn liked a good story, and when he heard one made a note of it. The diary contains two such stories. One is headed "Anecdot," and runs: "At a grand concert, as the director was about to begin the first number, the kettledrummer called loudly to him, asking him to wait a moment, because his two drums were not in tune. The leader could not and would not wait any longer, and told the drummer to transpose for the present." The second story is equally good. "An Archbishop of London, having asked Parliament to silence a preacher of the Moravian religion who preached in public, the Vice-President answered that could easily be done: only make him a Bishop, and he would keep silent all his life."

On the whole the note-book cannot be described as of strong biographical interest, but a reading of its contents as translated by Mr Krehbiel will certainly help towards an appreciation of the personal character of the composer.

CHAPTER VI

SECOND LONDON VISIT—1794-1795

HAYDN left London some time towards the end of June 1792. He had intended to visit Berlin, in response to an invitation from King Frederick William II, but he altered his route in order to meet Prince Anton Esterhazy, who was at Frankfort for the coronation of the Emperor Francis II. A more interesting meeting took place at Bonn. Beethoven, then a young man of twenty-two, was still living with his people in the Wenzegasse, but already arrangements had been made by the Elector for his paying a somewhat lengthened visit to Vienna in order to prosecute his studies there. Since the death of Mozart, Haydn had become the most brilliant star in the musical firmament, and it was only natural that the rising genius should look to him for no practical help and encouragement. It so happened that the Elector's Band, of which Beethoven was a member, gave a dinner to Haydn at Godesberg. The occasion was opportune. Beethoven submitted a cantata to the guest of the evening which Haydn "greatly praised, warmly encouraging the composer to proceed with his studies." The name of the cantata has not been ascertained, though Thayer conjectures it to have been on the death of the Emperor Leopold II.

Whatever it was, the fact of Haydn's approval would make it an easy matter to discuss the subject of lessons, whether now or later. Beethoven did not start for Vienna until November, and it appears that immediately before that date some formal communication had been made with Haydn in reference to his studies. On the 29th of October Count Waldstein wrote: "DEAR BEETHOVEN—You are travelling to Vienna in fulfilment of your long-cherished wish. The genius of Mozart is still weeping and bewailing the death of her favourite. With the inexhaustible Haydn she found a refuge, but no occupation, and is now waiting to leave him and join herself to someone else. Labour assiduously, and receive Mozart's spirit from the hands of Haydn." This was not exactly complimentary to Haydn, but Beethoven doubtless had the good sense not to repeat the count's words. When the young artist arrived in Vienna, he found Haydn living at the Hamberger Haus, No. 992 (since demolished), and thither he went for his lessons. From Beethoven's own notes of expenses we find that his first payment was made to Haydn on December 12. The sum entered is 8 groschen (about 9½d.), which shows at least that Haydn was not extravagant in his charges.

Beethoven's studies were in strict counterpoint, and the text-book was that same *Gradus ad Parnassum* of Fux which Haydn had himself contended with in the old days at St Stephen's. How many exercises Beethoven wrote cannot be said, but 245 have been preserved, of which, according to Nottebohm, Haydn corrected only forty-two. Much ink has been wasted in discussing the relations of these distinguished composers. There is no denying that Haydn neglected his young pupil, but one may find another excuse for the neglect besides that of his increasing age and his engrossing occupations. Beethoven was already a musical revolutionist: Haydn was content to walk in the old ways. The two men belonged almost to different centuries, and the disposition which the younger artist had for "splendid experiments" must have seemed to the mature musician little better than madness and licentious irregularity. "He will never do anything in decent style," was Albrechtsberger's dictum after giving Beethoven a series of lessons.

Haydn's opinion of Beethoven's future was not so dogmatically expressed; but he must have been sorely puzzled by a pupil who looked upon even consecutive fifths as an open question, and thought it a good thing to "learn occasionally what is according to rule that one may hereafter come to what is contrary to rule." It is said that Haydn persisted in regarding Beethoven, not as a composer at all but as a pianoforte player; and certainly Beethoven regarded Haydn as being behind the age. That he was unjust to Haydn cannot be gainsaid. He even went so far as to suspect Haydn of wilfully trying to retard him in his studies, a proceeding of which Haydn was altogether incapable. For many years he continued to discharge splenetic remarks about his music, and he was always annoyed at being called his pupil. "I never learned anything from Haydn," he would say; "he never would correct my mistakes." When, the day after the production of his ballet music to Prometheus, he met Haydn in the street, the old man observed to him: "I heard your music last night; I liked it very well." To which Beethoven, alluding to Haydn's oratorio, replied: "Oh! dear master, it is far from being a *creation*." The doubtful sincerity of this remark may be inferred from an anecdote quoted by Moscheles. Haydn had been told that Beethoven was speaking depreciatingly of "The Creation." "That is wrong of him," he said. "What has *he* written, then? His Septet? Certainly that is beautiful; nay, splendid."

It is hardly necessary to say who comes out best in these passages at arms. Yet we must not be too hard on Beethoven. That he recognised Haydn's genius as a composer no careful reader of his biography can fail to see. As Pohl takes pains to point out, he spoke highly of Haydn whenever opportunity offered, often chose one of his themes when improvising in public, scored one of his quartets for his own use, and lovingly preserved the autograph of one of the English symphonies. That he came in the end to realise his true greatness is amply proved by the story already related which represents him as exclaiming on his deathbed upon the fact of Haydn having been born in a common peasant's cottage.

In the meantime, although Beethoven was dissatisfied with his progress under Haydn, there was no open breach between the two. It is true that the young musician sought another teacher—one Schenck, a well-known Viennese composer—but this was done without Haydn's knowledge, out of consideration, we may assume, for his feelings. That master and pupil were still on the best of terms may be gathered from their having been at Eisenstadt together during the summer of 1793. In the January of the following year Haydn set out on his second visit to England, and Beethoven transferred himself to Albrechtsberger.

Haydn's life in Vienna during the eighteen months which intervened between the two London visits was almost totally devoid of incident. His wife, it will be remembered, had written to him in England, asking for money to buy a certain house which she fancied for a "widow's home." Haydn was astute enough not to send the money, but on his return to Vienna, finding the house in every way to his liking, he bought it himself. Frau Haydn died seven years later, "and now," said the composer, speaking in 1806, "I am living in it as a widower." The house is situated in the suburb of Vienna known as Gumpendorf. It is No. 19 of the Haydngasse and bears a marble memorial tablet, affixed to it in 1840. The pious care of the composer's admirers has preserved it almost exactly as it was in Haydn's day, and has turned it into a kind of museum containing portraits and mementoes of the master, the original manuscript of "The Creation," and other interesting relics.

Haydn started on his journey to England on January 19, 1794, Salomon having brought him under a promise to return with six new symphonies which he was to conduct in person. This time he travelled down the Rhine, and he had not been many days on the way when news reached him of the death of Prince Anton Esterhazy, who had very reluctantly given him leave of absence. On the occasion of the first London visit Salomon had been his travelling companion; now, feeling doubtless the encumbrance of increasing years, Haydn took his servant and copyist, Johann Elssler, along with him.

It may be noted in passing that he entertained a very warm regard for Elssler, whose father had been music copyist to Prince Esterhazy. He was born at Eisenstadt in 1769, and, according to Pohl, lived the whole of his life with Haydn, first as copyist, and then as general servant and factotum. It was Elssler who tended the composer in his last years, a service recompensed by the handsome bequest of 6000 florins, which he lived to enjoy until 1843. No man, it has been said, is a hero to his valet, but "Haydn was to Elssler a constant subject of veneration, which he carried so far that when he thought himself unobserved he would stop with the censer before his master's protrait as if it were the altar." This "true and honest servant" copied a large amount of Haydn's music, partly in score, partly in separate parts, much of which is now treasured as the autograph of Haydn, though the handwritings of the two are essentially different. It is a pity that none of the earlier writers on Haydn thought of applying to Elssler for particulars of the private life of the composer. He could have given information on many obscure points, and could have amplified the details of this second London visit, about which we know much less than we know about the former visit.

Salomon's first concert had been arranged for the 3rd of February, but Haydn did not arrive until the 4th, and the series accordingly began upon the 10th. Twelve concerts were given in all, and with the most brilliant success. The six new symphonies commissioned by Salomon were performed, and the previous set were also repeated, along with some new quartets. Of the many contemporary notices of the period, perhaps the most interesting is that which appears in the *Journal of Luxury and Fashion,* published at Weimar in July 1794. It is in the form of a London letter, written on March 25, under the heading of "On the Present State and Fashion of Music in England." After speaking of Salomon's efforts on behalf of classical music and of the praise due to him for his performance of the quartets of "our old favourite, Haydn," the writer continues: "But what would you now say to his new symphonies composed expressly for these concerts, and directed by himself at the piano? It is truly wonderful what sublime and august thoughts this master weaves into his works. Passages often occur which render it impossible to listen to them without becoming excited. We are altogether carried away by admiration, and forced to applaud with hand and mouth. This is especially the case with Frenchmen, of whom we have so many here that all public places are filled with them. You know that they have great sensibility, and cannot restrain their transports, so that in the midst of the finest passages in soft adagios they clap their hands in loud applause and thus mar the effect. In every symphony of Haydn the adagio or andante is sure to be repeated each time, after the most vehement encores. The worthy Haydn, whose personal acquaintance I highly value, conducts himself on these occasions in the most modest manner. He is indeed a good-hearted, candid, honest man, esteemed and beloved by all."

Several notable incidents occurred at the Salomon Concerts. It has been remarked, as "an event of some interest in musical history," that Haydn and Wilhelm Cramer appeared together at one concert, Cramer as leader of the orchestra, Haydn conducting from the pianoforte. But Cramer was not a genius of the first rank—his compositions are of the slightest importance—and there was nothing singular about his appearing along with Haydn. He had been leader at the Handel Festivals at Westminster Abbey in 1784 and 1787, and was just the man to be engaged for an enterprise like that of Salomon's. An anecdote told of Haydn in connection with one of the rehearsals is better worth noting. The drummer was found to be absent. "Can anyone here play the drum?" inquired Haydn, looking round from his seat at the piano. "I can," promptly replied young George (afterwards Sir George) Smart, who was sitting among the violinists.

Smart, who lived to become the *doyen* of the musical profession in England, had never handled a drumstick before, and naturally failed to satisfy the conductor. Haydn took the drumstick from him and "showed to the astonished orchestra a new and unexpected attitude in their leader." Then, turning to Smart, he remarked: "That is how we use the drumsticks in Germany." "Oh, very well," replied the unabashed youth, "if you like it better in that way we can also do it so in London."

Haydn made several new acquaintances during this visit, the most notable being, perhaps, Dragonetti, the famous double-bass player, who had accompanied Banti, the eminent *prima donna,* to London in 1794. Banti had been discovered as a *chanteuse* in a Paris *café,* and afterwards attracted much notice by her fine voice both in Paris and London. "She is the first singer in Italy, and drinks a bottle of wine every day," said one who knew her. In her journeys through Germany, Austria and Italy she won many triumphs. Haydn composed for her an air, "Non Partir," in E, which she sang at his benefit. As for "Old Drag," the familiar designation of the distinguished bassist, his eccentricities must have provided Haydn with no little amusement. He always took his dog Carlo with him into the orchestra, and Henry Phillips tells us that, having a strange weakness for dolls, he often carried one of them to the festivals as his wife! On his way to Italy in 1798 Dragonetti visited Haydn in Vienna, and was much delighted with the score of "The Creation," just completed. Several eminent violinists were in London at the time of Haydn's visit. The most distinguished of them was perhaps Felice de Giardini, who, at the age of fourscore, produced an oratorio at Ranelagh Gardens, and even played a concerto. He had a perfectly volcanic temper, and hated Haydn as the devil is said to hate holy water. "I don't wish to see the German dog," he remarked in the composer's hearing, when urged to pay him a visit. Haydn, as a rule, was kindly disposed to all brother artists, but to be called a dog was too much. He went to hear Giardini, and then got even with him by noting in his diary that he "played like a pig."

The accounts preserved of Haydn's second visit to England are, as already remarked, far less full than those of the first visit. Unconnected memoranda appear in his diary, some of which are given by Griesinger and Dies; but they are of comparatively little interest. During the summer of 1794 he moved about the country a good deal. Thus, about the 26th of August, he paid a visit to Waverley Abbey, whose "Annales Waverliensis" suggested to Scott the name of his first romance. The ruined condition of the venerable pile —it dates from 1128—set Haydn moralising on the "Protestant heresy" which led the "rascal mob " to tear down "what had once been a stronghold of his own religion." In the following month he spent three days in Bath with Dr Burney, and Rauzzini, the famous tenor, who had retired to the fashionable watering-place after a successful career of thirteen years as a singer and teacher in London. Rauzzini is little more than a name now, but for Haydn's sake it is worth recalling his memory. Born at Rome in 1747, his striking beauty of face and figure had drawn him into certain entanglements which made it expedient for him to leave his native land. He was as fond of animals as Dragonetti was of dolls, and had erected a memorial tablet in his garden to his "best friend," otherwise his dog. "Turk was a faithful dog and not a man," ran the inscription, which reminds one of Schopenhauer's cynical observation that if it were not for the honest faces of dogs, we should forget the very existence of sincerity. When Haydn read the inscription he immediately proceeded to make use of the words for a four-part canon. It was presumably at this time that he became acquainted with Dr Henry Harington, the musician and author, who had removed to Bath in 1771, where he had founded the Harmonic Society. Haydn dedicated one of his songs to him in return for certain music and verses, which explains the following otherwise cryptic note of Clementi's, published for the first time recently by Mr J. S. Shedlock: "The first Dr [Harington] having bestowed much praise on the second Dr [Haydn], the said second Dr, out of doctorial gratitude, returns the 1st Dr thanks for all favours reed, and praises in his turn the said 1st Dr most handsomely." The title of Haydn's song was "Dr Harington's Compliments."

The composer returned to London at the beginning of October for the winter season's concerts. These began, as before, in February, and were continued once a week up to the month of May. This time they took the form of opera concerts, and were given at the "National School of Music" in the new concert-room of the King's Theatre. No fresh symphonies were contributed by Haydn for this series, though some of the old ones always found a place in the programmes. Two extra concerts were given on May 21 and June 1, at both of which Haydn appeared; but the composer's last benefit concert was held on May 4. On this occasion the programme was entirely confined to his own compositions, with the exception of concertos by Viotti, the violinist, and Ferlendis, the oboist. Banti sang the aria already mentioned as having been written expressly for her, but, according to the composer, "sang very scanty." The main thing, however, was that the concert proved a financial success, the net receipts amounting to £400. "It is only in England," said Haydn, "that one can make 4000 gulden in one evening."

Haydn did indeed remarkably well in London. As Pohl says, "he returned from it with increased powers, unlimited fame, and a competence for life. By concerts, lessons, and symphonies, not counting his other compositions, he had again made £1200, enough to relieve him from all anxiety as to the future. He often said afterwards that it was not till he had been to England that he became famous in Germany; by which he meant that although his reputation was high at home, the English were the first to give him public homage and liberal remuneration."

It is superfluous to say that Haydn was as much of a "lion" in London society during his second visit as he had been on the previous occasion. The attention bestowed on him in royal circles made that certain, for "society" are sheep, and royalty is their bell-wether. The Prince of Wales had rather a fancy for him, and commanded his attendance at Carlton House no fewer than twenty-six times. At one concert at York House the programme was entirely devoted to his music. George III and Queen Caroline were present, and Haydn was presented to the King by the Prince. "You have written a great deal, Dr Haydn," said the King. "Yes, sire," was the reply; "more than is good for me." "Certainly not," rejoined His Majesty. He was then presented to the Queen, and asked to sing some German songs. "My voice," he said, pointing to the tip of his little finger, "is now no bigger than that"; but he sat down to the pianoforte and sang his song, " Ich bin der Verliebteste." He was repeatedly invited by the Queen to Buckingham Palace, and she tried to persuade him to settle in England. "You shall have a house at Windsor during the summer months," she said, and then, looking towards the King, added, "We can sometimes make music *tête-à-tête*." "Oh! I am not jealous of Haydn," interposed the King; "he is a good, honourable German." "To preserve that reputation," replied Haydn, "is my greatest pride."

Most of Haydn's appearances were made at the concerts regularly organised for the entertainment of royalty at Carlton House and Buckingham Palace, and Haydn looked to be paid for his services. Whether the King and the Prince expected him to give these services in return for the supposed honour they had conferred upon him does not appear. At all events, Haydn sent in a bill for 100 guineas sometime after his return to Vienna, and the amount was promptly paid by Parliament. Among the other attentions bestowed upon him while in London, mention should be made of the present of a talking parrot. Haydn took the bird with him, and it was sold for £140 after his death. Another gift followed him to Vienna. A Leicester manufacturer named Gardiner—he wrote a book on *The Music of Nature,* and other works—sent him half a dozen pairs of cotton stockings, into which were woven the notes of the Austrian Hymn, "My mother bids me bind my hair," the *Andante* from the "Surprise" Symphony, and other thematic material. These musical stockings, as a wit has observed, must have come as a *real* surprise to Haydn. It was this same Leicester manufacturer, we may remark parenthetically, who annotated the translation of Bombet's *Life of Haydn,* made by his fellow-townsman, Robert Brewin, in 1817.

Haydn's return from London was hastened by the receipt of a communication from Esterhaz. Prince Anton had been succeeded by his son Nicolaus, who was as fond of music as the rest of his family, and desired to keep his musical establishment up to the old standard. During the summer of 1794 he had written to Haydn, asking if the composer would care to retain his appointment as director. Haydn was only too glad to assent; and now that his London engagements were fulfilled, he saw no reason for remaining longer in England. Accordingly he started for home on the 15th of August 1795, travelling by way of Hamburg, Berlin and Dresden, and arriving at Vienna in the early days of September. Soon after his return he was surprised to receive an invitation to visit his native Rohrau. When he arrived there he found that a monument, with a marble bust of himself, had been erected to his honour in a park near his birth-place. This interesting memorial consists of a square pillar surmounting three stone steps, with an inscription on each side. The visit was produc-tive of mingled feelings to Haydn. He took his friends to see the old thatch-roofed cottage, and, pointing to the familiar stove, still in its place, modestly remarked that there his career as a musician began—a reminis-cence of the now far-away time when he sat by his father's side and sawed away on his improvised fiddle.

There is little to say about Haydn's labours as Capellmeister of the Esterhazy household at this time. Apparently he was only at Eisenstadt for the summer and autumn. Down to 1802, however, he always had a mass ready for Princess Esterhazy's name-day in September. These com-positions are Nos. 2, 1, 3, 16, 4 and 6 of the Novello edition. No. 2, Pohl tells us, was composed in 1796, and called the "Paukenmesse," from the fact of the drums being used in the *Agnus.* No. 3 was written in 1797. It is known in England as the Imperial Mass, but in Germany as "Die Nelsonmesse," on account of its having been performed during Nelson's visit to Eisenstadt in 1800. On that occasion Nelson asked Haydn for his pen, and gave him his own gold watch in exchange. It was shortly after his return to Vienna—in January 1797, to be precise—that he composed his favourite air, "God preserve the Emperor," better known as the Aus-trian Hymn. The story of this celebrated composition is worth telling with some minuteness. Its inception was due to Count von Saurau, Impe-rial High Chancellor and Minister of the Interior. Writing in 1820, the count said:

> I often regretted that we had not, like the English, a national air calcu-
> lated to display to all the world the loyal devotion of our people to the
> kind and upright ruler of our Fatherland, and to awaken within the hearts
> of all good Austrians that noble national pride so indispensable to the
> energetic fulfilment of all the beneficial measures of the sovereign. This
> seemed to me more urgent at a period when the French Revolution was

raging most furiously, and when the Jacobins cherished the idle hope of finding among the worthy Viennese partisans and participators in their criminal designs.[14] I caused that meritorious poet Haschka to write the words, and applied to our immortal countryman Haydn to set them to music, for I considered him alone capable of writing anything approaching in merit to the English 'God save the King.' Such was the origin of our national hymn."

It would not have been difficult to match "God save the King," the mediocrity of which, especially as regards the words, has been the butt of countless satirists. Beethoven wrote in his diary that he "must show the English what a blessing they have" in that "national disgrace." If Haydn regarded it as a "blessing," he certainly did not take it as a model. He produced an air which, looking at it from a purely artistic point of view, is the best thing of the national anthem kind that has ever been written. The Emperor was enchanted with it when sung on his birthday, February 12, 1797, at the National Theatre in Vienna, and through Count Saurau sent the composer a gold box adorned with a facsimile of the royal features. "Such a surprise and such a mark of favour, especially as regards the portrait of my beloved monarch," wrote Haydn, "I never before received in acknowledgement of my poor talents."

We have several indications of Haydn's predilection for this fine air, which has long been popular as a hymn tune in all the churches. He wrote a set of variations for it as the *Andante* of his "Kaiser Quartet." Griesinger tells us, too, that as often as the warm weather and his strength permitted, during the last few years of his life, he used to be led into his back room that he might play it on the piano. It is further related by Dies that, during the bombardment of Vienna in May 1809, Haydn seated himself at his instrument every forenoon to give forth the sound of the favourite song. Indeed, on May 26, only five days before his death, he played it over three times in succession, and "with a degree of expression that astonished himself." As one writer puts it, the air "seemed to have acquired a certain sacredness in his eyes in an age when kings were beheaded and their crowns tossed to the rabble."

Haydn's first sketch of the melody was found among his papers after his death. We reproduce it here with an improvement shown at the end. There are, it will be observed, some slight differences between the draft and the published version of the air:

The collecting of what Tennyson called "the chips of the workshop" is not as a rule an edifying business, but the evolution of a great national air must always be interesting.

It might perhaps be added that Dr Kuhac, the highest authority on Croatian folk-song, asserted in an article contributed to the *Croatian Review* (1893) that the Austrian National Hymn was based on a Croatian popular air. In reviewing Kuhac's collection of Croatian melodies, a work in four volumes, containing 1600 examples, Dr Reimann signifies his agreement with Kuhac, and adds that Haydn employed Croatian themes not only in "God preserve the Emperor," but in many passages of his other works. These statements must not be taken too seriously. Handel purloined wholesale from brother composers and said nothing about it. The artistic morality of Haydn's age was different, and, knowing his character as we do, we may be perfectly sure that if he had of set purpose introduced into any of his compositions music which was not his own he would, in some way or other, have acknowledged the debt. This hunting for plagiarisms which are not plagiarisms at all but mere coincidences— coincidences which are and must be inevitable—is fast becoming a nuisance, and it is the duty of every serious writer to discredit the practice. The composer of "The Creation" had no need to borrow his melodies from any source.

Chapter VII

"The Creation" and "The Seasons"

HAYDN rounded his life with "The Creation" and "The Seasons." They were the summit of his achievement, as little to be expected from him, considering his years, as "Falstaff" was to be expected from the octogenarian Verdi. Some geniuses flower late. It was only now, by his London symphonies and his "Creation," that Haydn's genius blossomed luxuriantly as to place him with almost amazing suddenness among the very first of composers. There is hardly anything more certain than this, that if he had not come to London he would not have stood where he stands to-day. The best of his symphonies were written for London; and it was London, in effect, that set him to work in what was for him practically a new direction, leading to the production of an oratorio which at once took its place by the side of Handel's master-pieces, and rose to a popularity second only to that of "The Messiah" itself.

The connection thus established between the names of Handel and Haydn is interesting, for there can be little question that Haydn was led to think of writing a large choral work chiefly as the result of frequently hearing Handel's oratorios during his visits to the metropolis. The credit of suggesting "The Creation" to Haydn is indeed assigned to Salomon, but it is more than probable that the matter had already been occupying his thoughts. It has been explicitly stated[15] that, being greatly impressed with the effect produced by "The Messiah," Haydn intimated to his friend Barthelemon his desire to compose a work of the same kind. He asked Barthelemon what subject he would advise for such a purpose, and Barthelemon, pointing to a copy of the Bible, replied: "There! take that, and begin at the beginning." This story is told on apparently good authority. But it hardly fits in with the statements of biographers. According to the biographers, Salomon handed the composer a libretto originally selected for Handel from Genesis and *Paradise Lost* by Mr Lidley or Liddell. That this was the libretto used by Haydn is certain, and we may therefore accept it as a fact that Haydn's most notable achievement in choral music was due in great measure to the man who had brought him to London, and had drawn from him the finest of his instrumental works.

Before proceeding further we may deal finally with the libretto of "The Creation." The "unintelligible jargon" which disfigures Haydn's immortal work has often formed the subject of comment; and assuredly nothing that can be said of it can well be too severe. "The Creation" libretto stands to the present day as an example of all that is jejune and incongruous in words for music. The theme has in itself so many elements of inspiration that it is a matter for wonder how, for more than a century, English-speaking audiences have listened to the arrant nonsense with which Haydn's music is associated. As has been well observed, "the suburban love-making of our first parents, and the lengthy references to the habits of the worm and the leviathan are almost more than modern flesh and blood can endure." Many years ago a leading musical critic wrote that there ought to be enough value, monetarily speaking, in "The Creation" to make it worth while preparing a fresh libretto; for, said he, "the present one seems only fit for the nursery, to use in connection with Noah's ark." At the Norwich Festival performance of the oratorio in 1872, the words were, in fact, altered, but in all the published editions of the work the text remains as it was. It is usual to credit the composer's friend, Baron van Swieten, with the "unintelligible jargon." The baron certainly had a considerable hand in the adaptation of the text. But in reality it owes its very uncouth verbiage largely to the circumstance that it was first translated from English into German, and then re-translated back into English; the words, with the exception of the first chorus, being adapted to the music. Considering the ways of translators, the best libretto in the world could not but have suffered under such transformations, and it is doing a real injustice to the memory of Baron Swieten, the good friend of more than one composer, to hold him up needlessly to ridicule.[16]

Haydn set to work on "The Creation " with all the ardour of a first love. Naumann suggests that his high spirits were due to the "enthusiastic plaudits of the English people," and that the birth of both "The Creation" and "The Seasons" was "unquestionably owing to the new man he felt within himself after his visit to England." There was now, in short, burning within his breast, "a spirit of conscious strength which he knew not he possessed, or knowing, was unaware of its true worth." This is somewhat exaggerated. Handel wrote "The Messiah" in twenty-four days; it took Haydn the best part of eighteen months to complete "The Creation," from which we may infer that "the sad laws of time" had not stopped their operation simply because he had been to London. No doubt, as we have already more than hinted, he was roused and stimulated by the new scenes and the unfamiliar modes of life which he saw and experienced in England. His temporary release from the fetters of official life had also an exhilarating influence. So much we learn indeed from himself. Thus, writing from London to Frau von Genzinger, he says: "Oh, my dear, good lady, how sweet is some degree of liberty! I had a kind prince, but was obliged at times to be dependent on base souls. I often sighed for freedom, and now I have it in some measure. I am quite sensible of this benefit, though my mind is burdened with more work. The consciousness of being no longer a bond-servant sweetens all my toils." If this liberty, this contact with new people and new forms of existence, had come to Haydn twenty years earlier, it might have altered the whole current of his career. But it did not help him much in the actual composition of "The Creation," which he found rather a tax, alike on his inspiration and his physical powers. Writing to Breitkopf & Härtel on June 12, 1799, he says: "The world daily pays me many compliments, even on the fire of my last works; but no one could believe the strain and effort it costs me to produce these, inasmuch as many a day my feeble memory and the unstrung state of my nerves so completely crush me to the earth, that I fall into the most melancholy condition, so much so that for days afterwards I am incapable of finding one single idea, till at length my heart is revived by Providence, when I seat myself at the piano and begin once more to hammer away at it. Then all goes well again, God be praised!"

In the same letter he remarks that, "as for myself, now an old man, I hope the critics may not handle my 'Creation' with too great severity, and be too hard on it. They may perhaps find the musical orthography faulty in various passages, and perhaps other things also which I have for so many years been accustomed to consider as minor points; but the genuine connoisseur will see the real cause as readily as I do, and will willingly cast aside such stumbling blocks." It is impossible to miss the significance of all this. Certainly it ought to be taken into account in any critical estimate of all this. Certainly it ought to be taken into account in any critical estimate of "The Creation;" for when a man admits his own shortcomings it is ungracious, to say the least, for an outsider to insist upon them. It is obvious at any rate that Haydn undertook the composition of the oratorio in no light-hearted spirit. "Never was I so pious," he says, "as when composing 'The Creation.' I felt myself so penetrated with religious feeling that before I sat down to the pianoforte I prayed to God with earnestness that He would enable me to praise Him worthily." In the lives of the great composers there is only one parallel to this frame of mind—the religious fervour in which Handel composed "The Messiah."

The first performance of "The Creation" was of a purely private nature. It took place at the Schwartzenburg Palace, Vienna, on the 29th of April 1798, the performers being a body of *dilettanti,* with Haydn presiding over the orchestra. Van Swieten had been exerting himself to raise a guarantee fund for the composer, and the entire proceeds of the performance, amounting to £350, were paid over to him. Haydn was unable to describe his sensations during the progress of the work. "One moment," he says, "I was as cold as ice, the next I seemed on fire; more than once I thought I should have a fit." A year later, on the 19th of March 1799, to give the exact date, the oratorio was first heard publicly at the National Theatre in Vienna, when it produced the greatest effect. The playbill announcing the performance (see next page) had a very ornamental border, and was, of course, in German.

Next year the score was published by Breitkopf & Härtel, and no fewer than 510 copies, nearly half the number subscribed for, came to England. The title-page was printed both in German and English, the latter reading as follows: "The Creation: an Oratorio composed by Joseph Haydn, Doctor of Musik, and member of the Royal Society of Musik, in Sweden, in actuel (*sic*) service of His Highness the Prince of Esterhazy, Vienna, 1800." Clementi had just set up a musical establishment in London, and on August 22, 1800, we find Haydn writing to his publishers to complain that he was in some danger of losing 2000 gulden by Clementi's non-receipt of a consignment of copies.

Salomon, strangely enough, had threatened Haydn with penalties for pirating his text, but he thought better of the matter, and now wrote to the composer for a copy of the score, so that he might produce the oratorio in London.

He was, however, forestalled by Ashley, who was at that time giving performances of oratorio at Covent Garden Theatre, and who brought forward the new work on the 28th of March (1800). An amusing anecdote is told in this connection. The score arrived by a King's messenger from Vienna on Saturday, March 22, at nine o'clock in the evening. It was handed to Thomas Goodwin, the copyist of the theatre, who immediately had the parts copied out for 120 performers. The performance was on the Friday evening following, and when Mr Harris, the proprietor of the theatre, complimented all parties concerned on their expedition, Goodwin, with ready wit, replied: "Sir, we have humbly emulated a great example; it is not the first time that the Creation has been completed in six days." Salomon followed on the 21st of April with a performance at the King's Theatre, Mara and Dussek taking the principal parts. Mara remarked that it was the first time she had accompanied an orchestra!

Strange to say—for oratorio has never been much at home in France— "The Creation" was received with immense enthusiasm in Paris when it was first performed there in the summer of this same year. Indeed, the applause was so great that the artists, in a fit of transport, and to show their personal regard for the composer, resolved to present him with a large gold medal. The medal was designed by the famous engraver, Gateaux. It was adorned on one side with a likeness of Haydn, and on the other side with an ancient lyre, over which a flame flickered in the midst of a circle of stars. The inscription ran: "Homage à Haydn par les Musiciens qui ont exécuté l'oratorio de la Création du Monde au Théâtre des Arts l'au ix de la République Française en MDCCC." The medal was accompanied by a eulogistic address, to which the recipient duly replied in a rather flowery epistle. "I have often," he wrote, "doubted whether my name would survive me, but your goodness inspires me with confidence, and the token of esteem with which you have honoured me perhaps justifies my hope that I shall not wholly die. Yes, gentlemen, you have crowned my grey hairs, and strewn flowers on the brink of my grave." Seven years after this Haydn received another medal from Paris— from the Société Académique des Enfants d'Apollon, who had elected him an honorary member.

A second performance of "The Creation" took place in the French capital on December 24, 1800, when Napoleon I escaped the infernal machine in the Rue Niçaise. It was, however, in England, the home of oratorio, that the work naturally took firmest root. It was performed at the Worcester Festival of 1800, at the Hereford Festival of the following year, and at Gloucester in 1802. Within a few years it had taken its place by the side of Handel's best works of the kind, and its popularity remained untouched until Mendelssohn's "Elijah" was heard at Birmingham in 1847. Even now, although it has lost something of its old-time vogue, it is still to be found in the repertory of our leading choral societies. It is said that when a friend urged Haydn to hurry the completion of the oratorio, he replied: "I spend much time over it because I intend it to

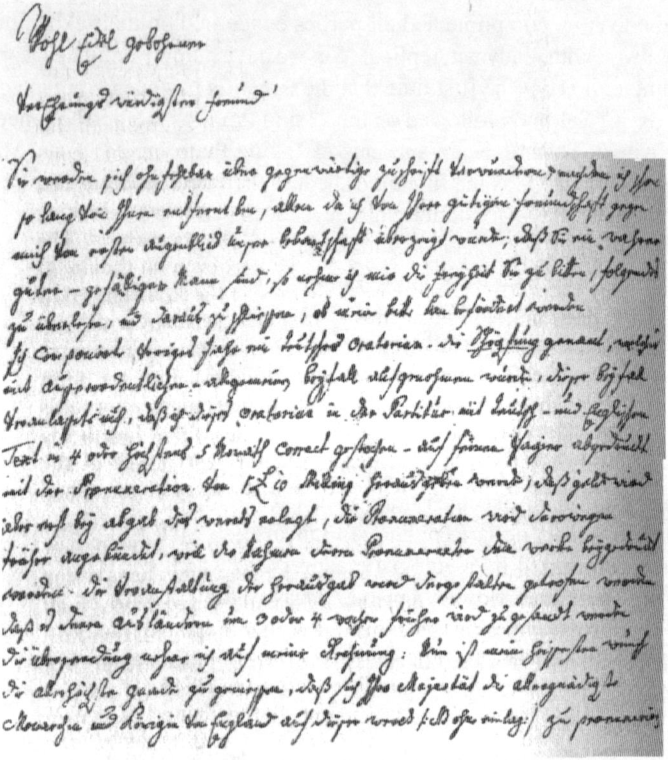

Facsimile of Letter Regarding "The Creation"

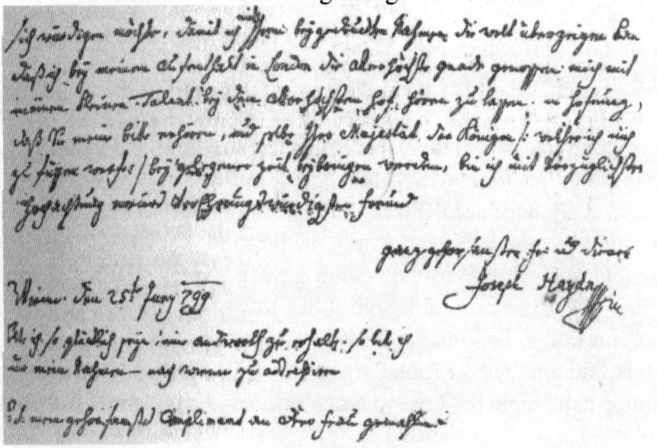

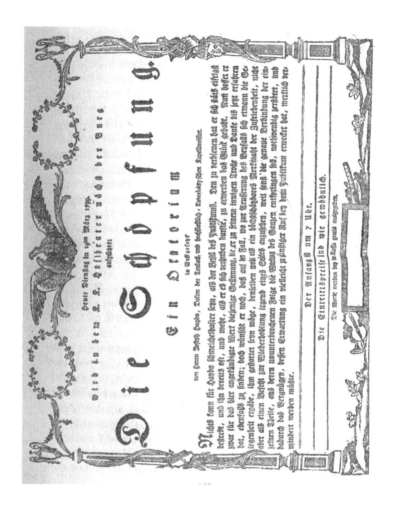

Facsimile of the Announcement Bill of the First Performance of "The Creation"

last a long time." How delighted he would have been could he have fore-
seen that it would still be sung and listened to with pleasure in the early
years of the twentieth century.

No one thinks of dealing critically with the music of "The Messiah;"
and it seems almost as thankless a task to take the music of "The Creation" to pieces. Schiller called it a "meaningless hotch-potch"; and even
Beethoven, though he was not quite innocent of the same thing himself,
had his sardonic laugh over its imitations of beasts and birds. Critics of
the oratorio seldom fail to point out these "natural history effects"—to
remark on "the sinuous motion of the worm," "the graceful gamboling of
the leviathan," the orchestral imitations of the bellowing of the "heavy
beasts," and such like. It is probably indefensible on purely artistic
grounds. But Handel did it in "Israel in Egypt" and elsewhere. And is
there not a crowing cock in Bach's "St Matthew Passion?" Haydn only
followed the example of his predecessors.

Of course, the dispassionate critic cannot help observing that there is
in "The Creation" a good deal of music which is finicking and something
which is trumpery. But there is also much that is first-rate. The instrumental representation of chaos, for example, is excellent, and nothing in
all the range of oratorio produces a finer effect than the soft voices at the
words, "And the Spirit of God moved upon the face of the waters." Even
the fortissimo C major chord on the word "light," coming abruptly after
the piano and mezzoforte minor chords, is as dazzling to-day as it was
when first sung. It has been said that the work is singularly deficient in
sustained choruses. That is true, if we are comparing it with the choruses
of Handel's oratorios. But Haydn's style is entirely different from that of
Handel. His choruses are designed on a much less imposing scale. They
are more reflective or descriptive, much less dramatic. It was not in his
way "to strike like a thunderbolt," as Mozart said of Handel. The descriptive effects which he desired to introduce into his orchestration made
it necessary that he should throw the vocal element into a simpler mould,
Allowance must be made for these differences. Haydn could never have
written "The Messiah," but, on the other hand, Handel could never have
written "The Creation."

The chief beauty of Haydn's work lies in its airs for the solo voices.
While never giving consummate expression to real and deep emotion,
much less sustained thought, they are never wanting in sincerity, and the
melody and the style are as pure and good as those of the best Italian
writing for the stage. With all our advance it is impossible to resist the

freshness of "With verdure clad," and the tender charm of such settings as that of "Softly purling, glides on, thro' silent vales, the limpid brook." On the whole, however, it is difficult to sum up a work like "The Creation," unless, as has been cynically remarked, one is prepared to call it great and never go to hear it. It is not sublime, but neither is it dull. In another fifty years, perhaps, the critic will be able to say that its main interest is largely historic and literary.[17]

After such an unexpected success as that of "The Creation," it was only in the nature of things that Haydn's friends should persuade him to undertake the composition of a second work of the kind. Van Swieten was insistent, and the outcome of his importunity was "The Seasons." This work is generally classed as an oratorio, but it ought more properly to be called a cantata, being essentially secular as regards its text, though the form and style are practically the same as those of "The Creation." The libretto was again due to Swieten, who, of course, adapted the text from James Thomson's well-known poem.

It would certainly have been a pity to lose such a fresh, melodious little work as "The Seasons;" but it is only too apparent that while there was no appreciable failure of Haydn's creative force, his physical strength was not equal to the strain involved by a composition of such length. In 1806, when Dies found him rather weaker than usual, he dolorously remarked: "You see it is all over with me. Eight years ago it was different, but 'The Seasons' brought on this weakness. I ought never to have undertaken that work. It gave me the finishing stroke." He appears to have started on the work with great reluctance and with considerable distrust of his own powers, but once fairly committed to the undertaking he entered into it with something of his old animation, disputing so manfully with his librettist over certain points in the text that a serious rupture between the two was at one time imminent. The subject was probably not very congenial to Haydn, who, as the years advanced, was more and more inclined towards devotional themes. That at least seems to be the inference to be drawn from the remark which he made to the Emperor Francis on being asked which of his two oratorios he himself preferred. "The Creation," answered Haydn. "In 'The Creation' angels speak and their talk is of God; in 'The Seasons' no one higher speaks than Farmer Simon."

But whether he liked the theme or not, in the end he produced a work as fresh and genial and melodious as if it had been the work of his prime. If anyone sees in it an evidence of weakness, he is seeing only what he had expected to see. Mr Rockstro remarks, not a trace of the "failing power" of which the grand old man complained is to be found in any part of it. It is a model of descriptive, contemplative work, and must please by its thoughtful beauty and illustrative power. True to Nature in its minutest details, it yet never insults her by trivial attempts at outward imitation where artistic suggestion of the hidden truth was possible. The "delicious softness" of the opening chorus, and the perfection of rustic happiness portrayed in the song which describes the joy of the "impatient husband man" are alone sufficient to prove that, whatever he may have thought about it himself, Haydn's genius was not appreciably waning.

The first performance of "The Seasons" took place at the Schwartzenburg Palace on the 24th of April 1801. It was repeated twice within a week; and on the 29th of May the composer conducted a grand public performance at the Redoutensaal. The work proved almost as successful as "The Creation." Haydn was enraptured with it, but he was never really himself again. As he said, it gave him the finishing stroke.

CHAPTER VIII

LAST YEARS

LITTLE is left to be told of the years which followed the production of "The Seasons." Haydn never really recovered from the strain which that last great effort of his genius had entailed. From his letters and the reminiscences of his friends we can read only too plainly the story of his growing infirmity. Even in 1799 he spoke of the diminution of his mental powers, and exclaimed: "Oh, God! how much yet remains to be done in this splendid art, even by a man like myself!" In 1802 he wrote of himself as "a gradually decaying veteran," enjoying only the feeble health which is "the inseparable companion of a grey-haired man of seventy." In December 1803 he made his last public exertion by conducting the "Seven Words" for the hospital fund at the Redoutensaal, and shortly afterwards wrote sadly of his "very great weakness." In 1804 he was asked to direct a performance of "The Creation," but declined on the score of failing strength. Gradually he withdrew himself almost entirely from the outside world, his general languor broken only by the visits of friends and by moods of passing cheerfulness. Cherubini, the Abbé Vogler, Pleyel, the Weber family, Hummel, Reichardt, and many others came to see him. Visits from members of the Esterhazy family gave him much pleasure. Mozart's widow also brought her son Wolfgang, to beg his blessing on the occasion of his first public concert in April 1805, for which he had composed a cantata in honour of Haydn's seventy-third birthday. But the homage of friends and admirers could not strengthen the weak hands or confirm the feeble knees. In 1806 Dies notes that his once-gleaming eye has become dull and heavy and his complexion sallow, while he suffers from "headache, deafness, forgetfulness and other pains." His old gaiety has completely gone, and even his friends have become a bore to him. "My remaining days," he said to Dies, "must all be spent in this lonely fashion . . . I have many visitors, but it confuses me so much to talk to them that at last I scarcely know what I am saying and only long to be left in peace." The condition of a man of naturally genial and optimistic temperament can easily be imagined from all this—

perhaps even more from the fact of his having a card printed to hand to inquirers who called, bearing the words:

Hin ist alle meine Kraft;
Alt und schwach bin ich.[18]

But while Haydn was thus suffering from the natural disabilities of his years, he was not wholly divorced from his art. It is true that nothing of any real importance came from his pen after "The Seasons," but a good deal of work of various kinds was done, some of which it is impossible for the biographer to ignore. One rather novel undertaking carries us back to the end of 1799, about which time he was first asked by George Thomson, the friend of Burns, to write accompaniments for certain Scottish songs to be published in Thomson's well - known national collections. The correspondence which followed is interesting in many ways, and as it is not noticed in any other biography of Haydn, we propose to deal with it here.[19]

George Thomson engaged at one time or other the services of Beethoven, Pleyel, Weber, Hummel, Bishop and Kozeluch. But Haydn was his first love. A genius of the kind, he writes in 1811, "never before existed and probably never will be surpassed." He is "the inimitable Haydn," the "delectable," the "father of us all," and so on. On the other hand, Haydn was proud of what he did for Thomson. "I boast of this work," he said, "and by it I flatter myself my name will live in Scotland many years after my death." Nay, if we may trust an authority cited by Thomson, so highly did he think of "the symphonies and accompaniments which he composed for my melodies as to have the original score of each framed and hung all over the walls of his bedroom." Little wonder that Thomson "loved the dear old man" and regretted that his worldly circumstances did not allow him to erect a statue to the composer at his own expense!

We have called this writing of symphonies and accompaniments for George Thomson a novel undertaking. It was, however, only novel in the sense of being rather out of Haydn's special "line." He had already been employed on work of the kind for the collection of William Napier, to which he contributed the accompaniments of 150 songs. Later on, too (in 1802-1803), he harmonised and wrote accompaniments for sixty-five airs, for which he received 500 florins from Whyte of Edinburgh.

The extent of his labours for George Thomson we shall now proceed to show.

Thomson addressed his first letter to Haydn in October 1799. There is no copy of it, but there is a copy of a letter to Mr Straton, a friend of Thomson's, who was at this time Secretary to the Legation at Vienna. Straton was to deliver the letter to Haydn, and negotiate with him on Thomson's behalf. He was authorised to "say whatever you conceive is likely to produce compliance," and if necessary to "offer a few more ducats for each air." The only stipulation was that Haydn "must not speak of what he gets." Thomson does not expect that he will do the accompaniments better than Kozeluch—"that is scarcely possible" (!); but in the symphonies he will be "great and original." Thomson, as we now learn from Straton, had offered 2 ducats for each air (say 20s.); Haydn "seemed desirous of having rather more than 2 ducats, but did not precisely insist upon the point." Apparently he did not insist, for the next intimation of the correspondence is to the effect that thirty-two airs which he had just finished had been forwarded to Thomson on June 19, 1800. They would have been done sooner, says Straton, but "poor Haydn laboured under so severe an illness during the course of this spring that we were not altogether devoid of alarm in regard to his recovery." Thomson, thus encouraged, sent sixteen more airs; and Straton writes (April 30, 1801) that Haydn at first refused to touch them because the price paid was too low. But in the course of conversation Straton learnt that Haydn was writing to Thomson to ask him to procure a dozen India handkerchiefs, and it struck him that "your making him a *present* of them might mollify the veteran into compliance respecting the sixteen airs." Straton therefore took upon himself to promise in Thomson's name that the handkerchiefs would be forthcoming, and "this had the desired effect to such a degree that Haydn immediately put the sixteen airs in his pocket, and is to compose the accompaniments as soon as possible on the same terms as the former."

The handkerchiefs duly arrived—"nice and large"—and Haydn made his acknowledgments in appropriate terms. At the same time (in January 1802) he wrote: "I send you with this the favourite air 'The Blue Bells of Scotland,' and I should like that this little air should be engraved all alone and dedicated in my name as a little complimentary gift to the renowned Mrs Jordan, whom, without having the honour of knowing, I esteem extremely for her great virtue and reputation." Mrs Jordan has been credited with the air of "The Blue Bells of Scotland." She certainly popularised the song, whether it was her own or not. In the note just quoted Haydn must have used the term "virtue" in the Italian sense.

After this a little hitch occurred in the Thomson correspondence. Haydn, being asked by Whyte, the publisher of a rival collection, to do something for his work, at once agreed. Thomson, not unnaturally, perhaps, felt hurt. He made his complaint through Mr Straton's successor at the Embassy, Mr Charles Stuart; and in August 1803 Stuart writes to say that he had broached the matter to Haydn "in as delicate terms as possible for fear he might take offence." Haydn frankly admitted that he had done the accompaniments for Whyte, but said the airs were different from those he had done for Thomson. After "a long conversation, he informed me," says Mr Stuart, "that being now seventy-four years of age and extremely infirm, he found himself wholly incapable of further application to study; that he must therefore beg leave to decline all offers, whether on your part or from any other person whatsoever. He even declared that notwithstanding the repeated requests of Prince Esterhazy, he felt himself utterly incapable of finishing several pieces of music he had undertaken, and being possessed of a competency he desired nothing so much as to pass the short time he has yet to live in repose and quiet." From this letter we learn that Thomson had unluckily sent a present of a handkerchief for Frau Haydn, who had now been dead for three years! In spite of the little misunderstanding just referred to Haydn was brought round once more, and on the 20th of December 1803 Thomson sends twenty-four airs, "which will most certainly be the last." Haydn's work delights him so much that he "really cannot bear the idea of seeking an inferior composer to finish a work already so nearly finished by you." He would pay 4 ducats for each air rather than have the mortification of a refusal. After this there is little of interest to note in the correspondence, unless it be a very "previous" letter of condolence which Thomson sent to Vienna. A false rumour had reached him that Haydn was dead. The following extract from a note which Haydn dictated to be sent to the friend who received Thomson's letter will explain the matter:

> Kindly say to Mr Thomson that Haydn is very sensible of the distress that the news of his alleged death has caused him, and that this sign of affection has added, if that were possible, to the esteem and friendship he will always entertain for Mr Thomson. You will notice that he has put his name and the date on the sheet of music to give better proof that he is still on this nether world. He begs you at the same time to be kind enough to have Mr Thomson's letter of condolence copied and to send him the copy.

Haydn's experience in this way was perhaps unique. Burney says he was reported dead in 1778; and the false rumour which reached Thomson in 1805 led Cherubini to compose a sacred cantata for three voices and orchestra, which was duly performed in Paris when his death actually occurred.

Haydn furnished in all some 250 airs with symphonies and accompaniments for Thomson. In the packet of letters from the composer, docketed by Thomson himself, the latter has placed a slip of paper indicating the various payments he had made. According to this statement Haydn had £291, 18s. for his work from first to last—not by any means an insignificant sum to make out of a side branch of his art.

This interesting correspondence takes us up to the year 1806, by which time Haydn's work was entirely over. His eventide, alas! was darkened by the clouds of war. The wave of the French Revolution had cast its bloody spray upon the surrounding nations, and 1805 saw the composer's beloved Vienna occupied by the French. Haydn was no politician, but love of country lay deep down in his heart, and he watched the course of events, from his little cottage, with the saddest forebodings. Once only was he drawn from his seclusion. This was on the 27th of March 1808, when he appeared in public for the last time at a performance of "The Creation" at the University. The scene on this remarkable occasion has been described by many pens. Naumann, writing of it, says that "such an apotheosis of the master was witnessed as has but few parallels," and this is no exaggeration. The performance, which was under the direction of Salieri, had been arranged in honour of his approaching seventy-sixth birthday. All the great artists of Vienna were present, among them Beethoven and Hummel. Prince Esterhazy had sent his carriage to bring the veteran to the hall, and, as he was being conveyed in an arm-chair to a place among the princes and nobles, the whole audience rose to their feet in testimony of their regard. It was a cold night, and ladies sitting near swathed him in their costly wraps and lace shawls. The concert began, and the audience was hushed to silence. When that magnificent passage was reached, "And there was light," they burst into loud applause, and Haydn, overcome with excitement, exclaimed, "Not I, but a Power from above created that."

The performance went on, but it proved too much for the old man, and friends arranged to take him home at the end of the first part. As he was being carried out, some of the highest of the land crowded round to take what was felt to be a last farewell; and Beethoven, forgetting incidents of early days, bent down and fervently kissed his hand and fore-head. Having reached the door, Haydn asked his bearers to pause and turn him towards the orchestra. Then, lifting his hand, as if in the act of blessing, he was borne out into the night.

Next year Vienna was bombarded by the French, and a cannon-ball fell not far from Haydn's house. He was naturally much alarmed; but there is no ground for the statement, sometimes made, that his death was hastened by the fright. On the contrary, he called out to his servants, who were assisting him to dress: "Children, don't be frightened; no harm can happen to you while Haydn is here." But his days were numbered. "This miserable war has cast me down to the very ground," he would say, with tears in his eyes. And yet it was a French officer who last visited him on his death-bed, the city, being then actually occupied by the enemy. The officer's name is not given, but he sang "In native worth" with such expression that Haydn was quite overcome, and embraced him warmly at parting. On May 26 he seems to have felt that his end was fast approaching. He gathered his household around him, and, being carried to the piano, at his own special request, played the Emperor's Hymn three times over, with an emotion that fairly overpowered himself and all who heard him. Five days later, on the 31st of May 1809, he breathed his last.

Funeral services were held in all the churches, and on June 15 Mozart's *Requiem* was given in his honour at the Scots Church, when several generals and administrators of the French army were present. Many poems were also written in his praise.

Haydn was buried as a private individual in the Hundsthurm Church-yard, which was just outside the lines, and close to the suburb of Gumpendorf, where he had lived. The grave remained entirely undistin-guished till 1814—another instance of Vienna's neglect—when Haydn's pupil, Chevalier Neukomm, erected a stone bearing an inscription, which contained a five-part canon for solution.

In 1820 the remains were exhumed by order of Prince Esterhazy, and re-interred with fresh funeral honours in the Pilgrimage Church of Maria-Einsiedel, near Eisenstadt, on November 7. A simple stone, with a Latin inscription, is inserted in the wall over the vault. When the coffin was opened, the startling discovery was made that the skull had been stolen. The desecration took place two days after the funeral. It appears that one Johann Peter, intendant of the royal and imperial prisons of Vienna, con-ceived the grim idea of forming a collection of skulls, made, as he avowed in his will, to corroborate the theory of Dr Gall, the founder of phrenology. This functionary bribed the sexton, and—in concert with Prince Esterhazy's secretary Rosenbaum, and with two Government officials named Jungermann and Ullmann—he opened Haydn's grave and removed the skull. Peter afterwards gave the most minute details of the sacrilege. He declared that he examined the head and found the bump of music fully developed, and traces in the nose of the polypus from which Haydn suffered. The skull was placed in a lined box, and when Peter got into difficulties and his collection was dispersed, the relic passed into the possession of Rosenbaum. That worthy's conscience seems to have troubled him in the matter, for he conceived the idea of erecting a monument to the skull in his back garden! When the desecration was discovered in 1820 there was an outcry, followed by police search. Prince Esterhazy would stand no nonsense. The skull must be returned, no questions would be asked, and Peter was offered a reward if he found it. The notion then occurred to Rosenbaum of palming off another skull for Haydn's. This he actually succeeded in doing, the head of some unfortunate individual being handed to the police. Peter claimed the reward, which was very justly refused him. When Rosenbaum was dying he confessed to the deception, and gave the skull back to Peter. Peter formed the resolution of bequeathing it, by will, to the Conservatorium at Vienna; but he altered his mind before he died, and by codicil left the skull to Dr Haller, from whose keeping it ultimately found its way to the anatomical museum at Vienna. We believe it is still in the museum. Its proper place is, of course, in Haydn's grave, and a stigma will rest on Vienna until it is placed there.[20]

A copy of Haydn's will has been printed as one of the appendices to the present volume, with notes and all necessary information about the interesting document. Two years before his death he had arranged that his books, music, manuscripts and medals should become the property of the Esterhazy family. Among the relics were twenty-four canons which had hung, framed and glazed, in his bedroom. "I am not rich enough," he said, "to buy good pictures, so I have provided myself with hangings of a kind that few possess." These little compositions were the subject of an oft-quoted anecdote. His wife, in one of her peevish moods, was complaining that if he should die suddenly, there was not sufficient money in the house to bury him. "In case such a calamity should occur," he replied, "take these canons to the music-publisher. I will answer for it that they will bring enough to pay for a decent funeral."

CHAPTER IX

HAYDN: THE MAN

SOMETHING of Haydn's person and character will have already been gathered from the foregoing pages. He considered himself an ugly man, and, in Addison's words, thought that the best expedient was "to be pleasant upon himself." His face was deeply pitted with small-pox, and the nose, large and aquiline, was disfigured by the polypus which he had inherited from his mother. In complexion he was so dark as to have earned in some quarters the familiar nickname of "The Moor." His underlip was thick and hanging, his jaw massive. "The mouth and chin are Philistine," wrote Lavater under his silhouette, noting, at the same time, "something out of the common in the eyes and the nose." The eyes were dark grey. They are described as "beaming with benevolence," and he used to say himself: "Anyone can see by the look of me that I am a good-natured sort of fellow."

In stature he was rather under the middle height, with legs disproportionately short, a defect rendered more noticeable by the style of his dress, which he refused to change with the changes of fashion. Dies writes: "His features were regular, his expression animated, yet, at the same time, temperate, gentle and attractive. His face wore a stern look when in repose, but in conversation "it was smiling and cheerful. I never heard him laugh out loud. His build was substantial, but deficient in muscle." Another of his aquaintances says that "notwithstanding a cast of physiognomy rather morose, and a short way of expressing himself, which seemed to indicate an ill-tempered man, the character of Haydn was gay, open and humorous." From these testimonies we get the impression of a rather unusual combination of the attractive and the repulsive, the intellectual and the vulgar. What Lavater described as the "lofty and good" brow was partly concealed by a wig, with side curls, and a pigtail, which he wore to the last. His dress as a private individual has not been described in detail, but the Esterhazy uniform, though frequently changing in colour and style, showed him in knee-breeches, white stockings, lace ruffles and white neckcloth. This uniform he never wore except when on actual duty.

After his death there were many portraits in chalks, engraved, and modelled in wax. Notwithstanding his admission of the lack of personal graces, he had a sort of feminine objection to an artist making him look old. We read that, in 1800, he was "seriously angry" with a painter who had represented him as he then appeared. "If I was Haydn at forty," said he, "why should you transmit to posterity a Haydn of seventy-eight?" Several writers mention a portrait by Sir Joshua Reynolds, and even give details of the sittings, but he never sat to Reynolds, whose eyesight had begun to fail before Haydn's arrival in England. During his first visit to London Hoppner painted his portrait at the special request of the Prince of Wales. This portrait was engraved by Facius in 1807 and is now at Hampton Court. Engravings were also published in London by Schiavonetti and Bartolozzi from portraits by Guttenbrunn and Ott, and by Hardy from his own oil-painting. A silhouette, which hung for long at the head of his bed, was engraved for the first time for Grove's Dictionary fo Music. This was said by Elssler, his old servant, to have been a striking likeness. Of the many busts, the best is that by his friend Grassi, the sculptor. Very little has been recorded of his social habits. Anything like excess in wine is not once mentioned; but it is easy to see from his correspondence that he enjoyed a good dinner, and was not insensible to creature comforts. Writing to Artaria from Esterhaz in 1788, he says: "By-the-by, I am very much obliged to you for the capital cheese you sent me, and also the sausages, for which I am your debtor, but shall not fail when an opportunity offers to return the obligation." In a subsequent letter to Frau von Genzinger he comically laments the change from Vienna to Esterhaz; "I lost twenty pounds in weight in three days, for the effect of my fare at Vienna disappeared on the journey. 'Alas! Alas!' thought I, when driven to eat at the *restaurateurs,* 'instead of capital beef, a slice of a cow fifty years old; instead of a ragout with little balls of force-meat, an old sheep with yellow carrots; instead of a Bohemian pheasant, a tough grill; instead of pastry, dry apple fritters and hazelnuts, etc.! Alas! Alas! Would that I now had many a morsel I despised in Vienna! Here in Esterhaz no one asks me, would you like some chocolate, with milk or without? Will you take some coffee, with or without cream? What can I offer you, my good Haydn? Will you have vanilla ice or pineapple?' If I had only a piece of good Parmesan cheese, particularly in Lent, to enable me to swallow more easily the black dumplings and puffs! I gave our porter this very day a commission to send me a couple of pounds." Even amid the social pleasures and excitements of London, where he was invited out six times a week and had "four excellent dishes" at every dinner, he longs to be back in his native land so that he may have "some good German soup."

We read that in Austria he "never associated with any but the musicians, his colleagues," a statement which cannot be strictly true. In London he was, as we have seen, something of a "lion," but it is doubtful if he enjoyed the conventional diversions of the *beau monde*. Yet he liked the company of ladies, especially when they were personally attractive. That he was never at a loss for a compliment may perhaps be taken as explaining his frequent conquests, for, as he frankly said himself, the pretty women "were at any rate not tempted by my beauty." Of children he was passionately fond, a fact which lends additional melancholy to his own unhappy and childless home life.

He was not highly educated, and he does not seem to have taken much interest in anything outside his own profession. This much may be gathered from his correspondence, upon which it is not necessary to comment at length. Mr Russell Lowell remarks that a letter which is not mainly about the writer loses its prime flavour. Haydn's letters are seldom "mainly about the writer." They help us very little in seeking to get at what Newman called "the inside of things," though some, notably those given at the end of this volume, embody valuable suggestions. He habitually spoke in the broad dialect of his native place. He knew Italian well and, French a little, and he had enough Latin to enable him to set the Church services. Of English he was almost entirely ignorant until he came to London in 1791, when we hear of him walking the country lanes with an English grammar in hand. There is an amusing story of a dinner at Madame Mara's, at which he was present during his first visit. Crossdill, the violon-cellist, proposed to celebrate him with "three times three." The suggestion was at once adopted, all the guests, with the exception of Haydn himself, standing up and cheering lustily. Haydn heard his name repeated, but not understanding what was going on, stared at the company in blank bewilderment. When the matter was explained to him he appeared quite overcome with diffidence, putting his hands before his face and not recovering his equanimity for some minutes.[21]

Of hobbies or recreations he appears to have had none, though, to relieve the dull monotony of life at Eisenstadt or Esterhaz, he occasionally indulged in hunting and fishing and mountain rambles. A leading trait in his character was his humour and love of fun. As he remarked to Dies: "A mischievous fit comes over me sometimes that is perfectly beyond control." The incident of the removal of the fellow chorister's pigtail will at once recur to the memory. The "Surprise" Symphony is another illustration, to say nothing of the "Toy" Symphony and "Jacob's Dream."

Of his generosity and his kindness to fellow artists there are many proofs. In 1800 he speaks of himself as having "willingly endeavoured all my life to assist everyone," and the words were no empty boast. No man was, in fact, more ready to perform a good deed. He had many needy relations always looking to him for aid, and their claims were seldom refused. A brother artist in distress was sure of help, and talented young men found in him a valuable friend, equally ready to give his advice or his gold, as the case might require. That he was sometimes imposed upon goes without saying. He has been charged with avarice, but the charge is wholly unfounded. He was simply careful in money matters, and that, to a large extent, because of the demands that were constantly being made upon him. In commercial concerns he was certainly sharp and shrewd, and attempts to take advantage of him always roused his indignation. "By heavens!" he writes to Artaria, "you have wronged me to the extent of fifty ducats . . . This step just cause the cessation of all transactions between us." The same firm, having neglected to answer some business proposition, were pulled up in this fashion: "I have been much provoked by the delay, inasmuch as I could have got forty ducats from another publisher for these five pieces, and you make too many difficulties about a matter by which, in such short compositions, you have at least a thirtyfold profit. The sixth piece has long had its companion, so pray make an end of the affair and send me either my music or my money."

The Haydn of these fierce little notes is not the gentle recluse we are apt to imagine him. They show, on the contrary, that he was not wanting in spirit when occasion demanded. He was himself upright and honest in all his dealings. And he never forgot a kindness, as more than one entry in his will abundantly testifies. He was absolutely without malice, and there are several instances of his repaying a slight with a generous deed or a thoughtful action. His practical tribute to the memory of Werner, who called him a fop and a "scribbler of songs," has been cited. His forbearance with Pleyel, who had allowed himself to be pitted against him by the London faction, should also be recalled; and it is perhaps worth mentioning further that he put himself to some trouble to get a passport for Pleyel during the long wars of the French Revolution. He carried his kindliness and gentleness even into "the troubled region of artistic life," and made friends where other men would have made foes.

His modesty has often been insisted upon. Success did not spoil him. In a letter of 1799 he asks that a certain statement in his favour should not be mentioned, lest he "be accused of conceit and arrogance, from which my Heavenly Father has preserved me all my life long." Here he spoke the simple truth. At the same time, while entirely free from presumption and vanity, he was perfectly alive to his own merits, and liked to have them acknowledged. When visitors came to see him nothing gave him greater pleasure than to open his cabinets and show the medals that had been struck in his honour, along with the other gifts he had received from admirers. Like a true man of genius, as Pohl says, he enjoyed distinction and fame, but carefully avoided ambition.

Of his calling and opportunities as an artist he had a very high idea. Acknowledging a compliment paid to him in 1802 by the members of the Musical Union in Bergen, he wrote of the happiness it gave him to think of so many families susceptible of true feeling deriving pleasure and enjoyment from his compositions. "Often when contending with the obstacles of every sort opposed to my work, often when my powers both of body and mind failed, and I felt it a hard matter to persevere in the course I had entered on, a secret feeling within me whispered, 'There are but few contented and happy men here below; everywhere grief and care prevail, perhaps your labours may one day be the source from which the weary and worn or the man burdened with affairs may derive a few moments' rest and refreshment.' What a powerful motive to press onwards! And this is why I now look back with heartfelt, cheerful satisfaction on the work to which I have devoted such a long succession of years with such persevering efforts and exertions."

With this high ideal was combined a constant effort to perfect himself in his art. To Kalkbrenner he once made the touching remark: "I have only just learned in my old age how to use the wind instruments, and now that I do understand them I must leave the world." To Griezinger, again, he said that he had by no means exhausted his genius: that "ideas were often floating in his mind, by which he could have carried the art far beyond anything it had yet attained, had his physical powers been equal to the task." Closely, indeed inseparably, connected with this exalted idea of his art was his simple and sincere piety. He was a devout Christian, and looked upon his genius as a gift from God, to be freely used in His service. His faith was never assailed with doubts; he lived and died in the communion of the Catholic Church, and was "never in danger of becoming either a bigot or a free-thinker." When Carpani, anticipating latter-day criticism, hinted to him that his Church compositions were impregnated with a light gaiety, he replied: "I cannot help it; I give forth what is in me. When I think of the Divine Being, my heart is so full of joy that the notes fly off as from a spindle, and as I have a cheerful heart He will pardon me if I serve Him cheerfully."

His reverent practice during the composition of "The Creation" has been mentioned. "Never was I so pious," he said. There are many proofs of the same feeling in his correspondence and other writings. Thus he concludes an autobiographical sketch with the words: "I offer up to Almighty God all eulogiums, for to Him alone do I owe them. My sole wish is neither to offend against my neighbour nor my gracious prince, but above all not against our merciful God." Again, in one of his later letters, he says: "May God only vouchsafe to grant me the health that I have hitherto enjoyed, and may I preserve it by good conduct, out of gratitude to the Almighty." The note appended to the first draft of his will is also significant. Nor in this connection should we forget the words with which he inscribed the scores of his more important compositions. For the conclusion he generally adopted Handel's *Soli Deo Gloria* or *Laus Deo,* with the occasional addition of *et B. V. Mae. et Oms. Sis. (Beatae Virgini Mariae et Omnibus Sanctis).* Even his opera scores were so inscribed, one indeed having the emphatic close: *Laus omnipotenti Deo et Beatissimae Virgini Mariae.* The superscription was uniformly *In nomine Domini.* It is recorded somewhere that when, in composing, he felt his inspiration flagging, or was baulked by some difficulty, he rose from the instrument and began to run over his rosary. In short, not to labour the point, he had himself followed the advice which, as an old man, he gave to the choirboys of Vienna: "Be good and industrious and serve God continually."

The world has seen many an instance of genius without industry, as of industry without genius. In Haydn the two were happily wedded. He was always an early riser, and long after his student days were over he worked steadily from sixteen to eighteen hours a day. He lived strictly by a self-imposed routine, and was so little addicted to what Scott called "bedgown and slipper tricks," that he never sat down to work or received a visitor until he was fully dressed. He had none of Wagner's luxurious tastes or Balzac's affectations in regard to a special attire for work, but when engaged on his more important compositions he always wore the ring given him by the King of Prussia. In Haydn's case there are no incredible tales of dashing off scores in the twinkling of an eye. That he produced so much must be attributed to his habit of devoting all his leisure to composition. He was not a rapid worker if we compare him with Handel and Mozart. He never put down anything till he was "quite sure it was the right thing"—a habit of mind indicated by his neat and uniform handwriting[22]—and he assures us: "I never was a quick writer, and always composed with care and deliberation. That alone," he added, " is the way to compose works that will last, and a real connoisseur can see at a glance whether a score has been written in undue haste or not." He is quoted as saying that "genius is always prolific." However the saying may be interpreted, there does not seem to have been about him anything of what has been called the irregular *déshabillé* of composers, "the natural result of the habit of genius of watching for an inspiration, and encouraging it to take possession of the whole being when it comes."

His practice was to sketch out his ideas roughly in the morning, and elaborate them in the afternoon, taking pains to preserve unity in idea and form. "That is where so many young composers fail," he said in reference to the latter point. "They string together a number of fragments; they break off almost as soon as they have begun, and so at the end the listener carries off no definite impression." The importance of melody he specially emphasised. "It is the air which is the charm of music," he remarked, "and it is that which is most difficult to produce. The invention of a fine melody is the work of genius." In another place he says: "In vocal composition, the art of producing beautiful melody may now almost be considered as lost; and when a composer is so fortunate as to throw forth a passage that is really melodious, he is sure, if he be not sensible of its excellence, to overwhelm and destroy it by the fullness and superfluity of his instrumental parts."[23]

He is stated to have always composed with the aid of the pianoforte or harpsichord; and indeed we find him writing to Artaria in 1788 to say that he has been obliged to buy a new instrument "that I might compose your clavier sonatas particularly well." This habit of working out ideas with the assistance of the piano has been condemned by most theorists as being likely to lead to fragmentariness. With Haydn at anyrate the result was entirely satisfactory, for, as Sir Hubert Parry points out, the neatness and compactness of his works is perfect. It is very likely, as Sir

Hubert says, that most modern composers have used the pianoforte a good deal—not so much to help them to find out their ideas, as to test the details and intensify their musical sensibility by the excitant sounds, the actual sensual impression of which is, of course, an essential element in all music. The composer can always hear such things in his mind, but obviously the music in such an abstract form can never have quite as much effect upon him as when the sounds really strike upon his ear.[24]

Like all the really great composers, Haydn was no pedant in the matter of theoretical formulae, though he admitted that the rigid rules of harmony should rarely be violated, and "never without the compensation of some inspired effect." When he was asked according to what rule he had introduced a certain progression, he replied: "The rules are all my very obedient humble servants." With the quint-hunters and other faddists who would place their shackles on the wrists of genius, he had as little patience as Beethoven, who, when told that all the authorities forbade the consecutive fifths in his C Minor Quartet, thundered out: "Well, I allow them." Somebody once questioned him about an apparently unwarranted passage in the introduction to Mozart's Quartet in C Major. "If Mozart has written it, be sure he had good reasons for doing so," was the conclusive reply. That fine old smoke-dried pedant, Albrechtsberger, declared against consecutive fourths in strict composition, and said so to Haydn. "What is the good of such rules?" demanded Haydn. "Art is free and must not be fettered by mechanical regulations. The cultivated ear must decide, and I believe myself as capable as anyone of making laws in this respect. Such trifling is absurd; I wish instead that someone would try to compose a really new minuet." To Dies he remarked further: "Supposing an idea struck me as good and thoroughly satisfactory both to the ear and the heart, I would far rather pass over some slight grammatical error than sacrifice what seemed to me beautiful to any mere pedantic trifling." These were sensible views. Practice must always precede theory. When we find a great composer infringing some rule of the old text-books, there is, to say the least, a strong presumption, not that the composer is wrong, but that the rule needs modifying. The great composer goes first and invents new effects: it is the business of the theorist not to cavil at every novelty, but to follow modestly behind and make his rules conform to the practice of the master.[25]

Thus much about Haydn the man. Let us now turn to Haydn the composer and his position in the history of music.

CHAPTER X

HAYDN: THE COMPOSER

HAYDN has been called "the father of instrumental music," and although rigid critics may dispute his full right to that title, on broad grounds he must be allowed to have sufficiently earned it. He was practically the creator of more than one of our modern forms, and there was hardly a department of instrumental music in which he did not make his influence felt. This was emphatically the case with the sonata, the symphony and the string quartet.

The latter he brought to its first perfection. Before his time this particular form of chamber music was long neglected, and for a very simple reason. Composers looked upon it as being too slight in texture for the display of their genius. That, as has often been demonstrated, was because they had not mastered the art of "writing a four-part harmony with occasional transitions into the pure polyphonic style—a method of writing which is indispensable to quartet composition—and also because they did not yet understand the scope and value of each individual instrument."

It would be too much to say that even Haydn fully realised the capacities of each of his four instruments. Indeed, his quartet writing is often bald and uninteresting. But at least he did write in four-part harmony, and it is certainly to him that we owe the installation of the quartet as a distinct species of chamber music. "It is not often," says Otto Jahn, the biographer of Mozart, "that a composer hits so exactly upon the form suited to his conceptions; the quartet was Haydn's natural mode of expressing his feelings." This is placing the Haydn quartet in a very high position among the products of its creator. But its artistic value and importance cannot well be over-estimated. Even Mozart, who set a noble seal upon the form, admitted that it was from Haydn he had first learned the true way to compose quartets; and there have been enthusiasts who regarded the Haydn quartet with even more veneration than the Haydn symphony. No fewer than seventy-seven quartets are ascribed to him. Needless to say, they differ considerably as regards their style and treatment, for the first was written so early as 1755, while the last belongs to his later years. But they are all characterised by the same combination of manly earnestness, rich invention and mirthful spirit. The form is concise and symmetrical, the part-writing is clear and well-balanced, and a "sunny sweetness" is the prevailing mood. As a discerning critic has remarked, there is nothing in the shape of instrumental music much pleasanter and easier to listen to than one of Haydn's quartets. The best of them hold their places in the concert-rooms of to-day, and they seem likely to live as long as there are people to appreciate clear and logical composition which attempts nothing beyond "organised simplicity."[26] In this department, as Goethe said, he may be superseded, he can never be surpassed.

For the symphony Haydn did no less than for the quartet. The symphony, in his young days, was not precisely the kind of work which now bears the name. It was generally written for a small band, and consisted of four parts for strings and four for wind instruments. It was meant to serve no higher purpose, as a rule, than to be played in the houses of nobles; and on that account it was neither elaborated as to length nor complicated as to development. So long as it was agreeable and likely to please the aristocratic ear, the end of the composer was thought to be attained.

Haydn, as we know, began his symphonic work under Count Morzin. The circumstances were not such as to encourage him to "rise to any pitch of real greatness or depth of meaning;" and although he was able to build on a somewhat grander scale when he went to Eisenstadt, it was still a little comfortable *coterie* that he understood himself to be writing for rather than for the musical world at large. Nevertheless, he aimed at constant improvement, and although he had no definite object in view, he "raised the standard of symphony—writing far beyond any point which had been attained before." "His predecessors," to quote Sir Hubert Parry, "had always written rather carelessly and hastily for the band, and hardly ever tried to get refined and original effects from the use of their instruments, but he naturally applied his mind more earnestly to the matter in hand, and found out new ways of contrasting and combining the tones of different members of his orchestra, and getting a fuller and richer effect out of the mass of them when they were all playing. In the actual style of the music, too, he made great advances, and in his hands symphonies became by degrees more vigorous, and, at the same time, more really musical." But the narrow limits of the Esterhazy audience and the numbing routine of the performances were against his rising to the top heights of his genius.

It was only when he came to write for the English public that he showed what he could really do with the matter of the symphony. In comparison with the twelve symphonies which he wrote for Salomon, the other, and especially the earlier works are of practically no account. They are interesting, of course, as marking stages in the growth of the symphony and in the development of the composer's genius. But regarded in themselves, as absolute and individual entities, they are not for a moment to be placed by the side of the later compositions. These, so far as his instrumental music is concerned, are the crowning glory of his life work. They are the ripe fruits of his long experience working upon the example of Mozart, and mark to the full all those qualities of natural geniality, humour, vigour and simple good-heartedness, which are the leading characteristics of his style.

Haydn's sonatas show the same advance in form as his symphonies and quartets. The older specimens of the sonata, as seen in the works of Fiber, Kuhnau, Mattheson and others, contain little more than the germs of the modern sonata. Haydn, building on Emanuel Bach, fixed the present form, improving so largely upon the earlier, that we could pass from his sonatas directly to those of Beethoven without the intervention of Mozart's as a connecting link. Beethoven's sonatas were certainly more influenced by Haydn's than by Mozart's. Haydn's masterpieces in this kind, like those of Mozart and Beethoven, astonish by their order, regularity, fluency, harmony and roundness; and by their splendid development into full and complete growth out of the sometimes apparently unimportant germs.[27] Naturally his sonatas are not all masterpieces. Of the thirty-five, some are old-fashioned and some are quite second-rate. But, like the symphonies, they are all of historical value as showing the development not only of the form but of the composer's powers. One of the number is peculiar in having four movements; another is equally peculiar—to Haydn at least—in having only two movements. Probably in the case of the latter the curtailment was due to practical rather than to artistic reasons. Like Beethoven, with the two-movement sonata in C minor, Haydn may not have had time for a third! In several of the sonatas the part-writing strikes one as being somewhat poor and meagre; in others there is, to the modern ear, a surfeiting indulgence in those turns, arpeggios and other ornaments which were inseparable from the nature of the harpsichord, with its thin tones and want of sustaining power. If Haydn had lived to write for the richer and more sustained sounds of the modern pianoforte, his genius would no doubt have responded to the increased demands made upon it, though we may doubt whether it was multiplex enough or intellectual enough to satisfy the deeper needs of our time. As it is, the changes which have been made in sonata form since his day are merely changes of detail. To him is due the fixity of the form.[28]

Of his masses and Church music generally it is difficult to speak critically without seeming unfair. We have seen how he explained what must be called the almost secular style of these works. But while it is true that Haydn's masses have kept their place in the Catholic churches of Germany and elsewhere, it is impossible, to Englishmen, at any rate, not to feel a certain incongruity, a lack of that dignity and solemnity, that religious "sense," which makes our own Church music so impressive. We must not blame him for this. He escaped the influences which made Bach and Handel great in religious music—the influences of Protestantism, not to say Puritanism. The Church to which he belonged was no longer guided in its music by the principles of Palestrina. On the contrary, it was tainted by secular and operatic influences; and although Haydn felt himself to be thoroughly in earnest it was rather the ornamental and decorate side of religion that he expressed in his lively music. He might, perhaps, have written in a more serious, lofty strain had he been brought under the noble traditions which glorified the sacred choral works of the earlier masters just named. In any case, his Church music has nothing of the historical value of his instrumental music. It is marked by many sterling and admirable qualities, but the progress of the art would not have been materially affected if it had never come into existence.

As a song-writer Haydn was only moderately successful, perhaps because, having himself but a slight acquaintance with literature, he left the selection of the words to others, with, in many cases, unfortunate results. The form does not seem to have been a favourite with him, for his first songs were not produced until so late as 1780. Some of the later compositions have, however, survived; and one or two of the canzonets, such as "My mother bids me bind my hair" and "She never told her love," are admirable. The three-part and the four-part songs, as well as the canons, of which he thought very highly himself, are also excellent, and still charm after the lapse of so many years.

On the subject of his operas little need be added to what has already been said. Strictly speaking, he never had a chance of showing what he could do with opera on a grand scale. He had to write for a small stage

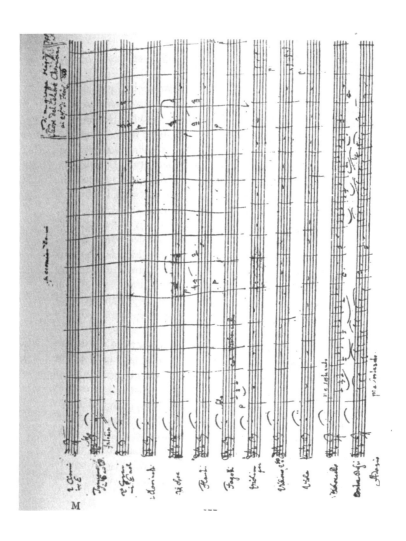

and a small audience, and in so far he was probably successful. Pohl thinks that if his project of visiting Italy had been fulfilled and his faculties been stimulated in this direction by fresh scenes and a larger horizon, we might have gained "some fine operas." It is doubtful. Haydn lacked the true dramatic instinct. His placid, easy-going, contented nature could never have allowed him to rise to great heights of dramatic force. He was not built on a heroic mould; the meaning of tragedy was unknown to him.

Regarding his orchestration a small treatise might be written. The terms which best describe it are, perhaps, refinement and brilliancy. Much of his success in this department must, of course, be attributed to his long and intimate association with the Esterhazy band. In 1766, six years after his appointment, this band numbered seventeen instrument—six violins and viola, one violoncello, one double bass, one flute, two oboes, two bassoons and four horns. It was subsequently enlarged to twenty-two and twenty-four, including trumpets and kettledrums on special occasions. From 1776 to 1778 there were also clarinets. This gradual extension of resources may be taken as roughly symbolising Haydn's own advances in the matter of orchestral development. When he wrote his first symphony in 1759 he employed first and second violins, violas, basses, two oboes and two horns; in his last symphony, written in 1795, he had at his command "the whole symphonic orchestra as it had stood when Beethoven took up the work of orchestral development." Between these two points Mozart had lived and died, leaving Haydn his actual debtor so far as regards the increased importance of the orchestra. It has been said that he learnt from Mozart the use of the clarinet, and this is probably true, notwithstanding the fact that he had employed a couple of clarinets in his first mass, written in 1751 or 1752. Both composers used clarinets rarely, but Haydn certainly did not reveal the real capacity of the instrument or establish its position in the orchestra as Mozart did.

From his first works onwards, he proceeded along the true symphonic path, and an orchestra of two flutes, two oboes, two clarinets, two bassoons, two horns, two trumpets, drums, and the usual strings fairly represents the result of his contributions to its development up to the first successful experiments of Mozart. The names of Mozart and Haydn ought in reality to be coupled together as the progenitors of the modern orchestral colouring. But the superiority must be allowed to attach to Haydn, inasmuch as his colouring is the more expansive and decided. Some of his works, even of the later period, show great reticence in scoring, but, on the other hand, as in "The Creation," he knew when to draw upon the full resources of the orchestra. It has been pointed out as worthy of remark that he was not sufficiently trustful of his instrumental army to leave it without the weak support of the harpsichord, at which instrument he frequently sat during the performance of his symphonies, and played with the orchestra, with extremely bad effect.[29] In this, however, he merely followed the custom of his day.

Of Haydn's general style as a composer it is hardly necessary to speak. To say that a composition is "Haydnish" is to express in one word what is well understood by all intelligent amateurs. Haydn's music is like his character—clear, straightforward, fresh and winning, without the slightest trace of affectation or morbidity. Its perfect transparency, its firmness of design, its fluency of instrumental language, the beauty and inexhaustible invention of its melody, its studied moderation, its child-like cheerfulness—these are some of the qualities which mark the style of this most genial of all the great composers.

That he was not deep, that he does not speak a message of the inner life to the latter-day individual, who, in the Ossianic phrase, likes to indulge in "the luxury of grief," must, of course, be admitted. The definite embodiment of feeling which we find in Beethoven is not to be found in him. It was not in his nature. "My music," says Schubert, "is the production of my genius and my misery." Haydn, like Mendelssohn, was never more than temporarily miserable. But in music the gospel of despair seldom wants its preachers. To day it is Tschaikowsky, tomorrow it will be another. Haydn meant to make the world happy, not to tear it with agony. "I know," he said, "that God has bestowed a talent upon me, and I thank Him for it. I think I have done my duty, and been of use in my generation by my works. Let others do the same."

Appendix A

HAYDN'S LAST WILL AND
TESTAMENT

THE following draft of Haydn's will is copied from Lady Wallace's *Letters of Distinguished Musicians* (London, 1867), where it was published in full for the first time. The much-corrected original is in the Court Library at Vienna. Dies says: "Six weeks before his death, in April 1809, he read over his will to his servants in the presence of witnesses, and asked them whether they were satisfied with his provisions or not. The good people were quite taken by surprise at the kindness of their master's heart, seeing themselves thus provided for in time to come, and they thanked him with tears in their eyes." The extracts given by Dies vary in some particulars from the following, because Haydn's final testamentary dispositions were made at a later date. But, as Lady Wallace says, it is not the legal but the moral aspect of the affair that interests us. Here we see epitomised all the goodness and beauty of Haydn's character. The document runs as follows:

1. For holy masses, 12 florins
2. To the Norman School, 5
3. To the Poorhouse, 5
4. To the executor of my will, 200
    And also the small portrait of Grassi.
5. To the pastor, 10
6. Expenses of my funeral, first-class, 200
7. To my dear brother Michael, in Salzburg, 4000
8. To my brother Johann, in Eisenstadt, 4000
9. To my sister in Rohrau (erased, and written underneath): "God have mercy on her soul! To the three children of my sister," 2000
10. To the workwoman in Esterhazy, Anna Maria Moser, *née* Fröhlichin, 500
11. To the workwoman in Rohrau, Elisabeth, *née* Böhme, 500

12. To the two workwomen there (erased, and replaced by: "To the shoe-
    maker, Anna Loder, in Vienna")
    Should she presume to make any written claims, I declare them to
    be null and void, having already paid for her and her profligate hus-
    band, Joseph Lungmayer, more than 6000 gulden.
13. To the shoemaker in Garhaus, Theresa Hammer, 500
14. To her son, the blacksmith, Matthias Frohlich, 500
15. To the eldest child of my deceased sister, Anna Wimmer, and her
    husband, at Meolo, in Hungary, 500
17. To her married daughter at Kaposwar, 100
18. To the other three children (erased), 300
19. To the married Düsse, *née* Scheeger, 300
20. To her imbecile brother, Joseph (erased), 100
21. To her brother, Karl Scheeger, silversmith, and his wife, 900
23. To the son of Frau von Koller, 300
23. To his son (erased), 100
24. To the sister of my late wife (erased).
25. To my servant, Johann Elssler, 2500
    Also one year's wages, likewise a coat, waistcoat and a pair of
    trousers. (According to Griesinger, Haydn bequeathed a capital of
    6000 florins to this faithful servant and copyist.)
26. To Rosalia Weber, formerly in my service. (She has a written certifi-
    cate of this from me), 300
27. To my present maid-servant, Anna Kremnitzer, 1000
    And a year's wages in addition. Also, her bed and bedding and
    two pairs of linen sheets; also, four chairs, a table, a chest of
    drawers, the watch, the clock and the picture of the Blessed Virgin
    in her room, a flat-iron, kitchen utensils and crockery, one water-
    pail, and other trifles.
28. To my housekeeper, Theresia Meyer, 500
    And one year's wages, 20
29. To my old gardener, Michel, 24
30. To the Prince's Choir for my obsequies, to share alike (erased), 100
31. To the priest (erased), 12
32. To the pastor in Eisenstadt for a solemn mass, 5
33. To his clerk, 2
34. To the beneficiary, 2
35. To Pastor von Nollendorf, 2
36. To Pastor von St Georg, 2

37. To the sexton (erased from 33), 1
38. To the organ-bellows' blower, 1
39. To the singer, Babett, 50
40. To my cousin, the saddler's wife, in Eisenstadt, 50
    To her daughter, 300
41. To Mesdemoiselles Anna and Josepha Dillin, 100
42. To the blind daughter of Herr Graus, leader of the choir in Eisenstadt (erased), 100
43. To the four sisters Sommerfeld, daughters of the wigmaker in Presburg, 200
44. To Nannerl, daughter of Herr Weissgerb, my neighbour (erased), 50
45. To Herr Art, merchant in the Kleine Steingasse, 50
46. To the pastor in Rohrau, 12
47. To the schoolmaster in Rohrau, 6
48. To the school children, 3
49. To Herr Wamerl, formerly with Count v. Harrach, 50
50. To his present cashier, 50
51. To Count v. Harrach for the purpose of defraying the bequests Nos. 51 and 52, I bequeath an obligation of 6000 florins at 5 per cent., the interest to be disposed of as follows:

    To the widow Aloysia Polzelli, formerly singer at Prince Nikolaus Esterhazy's, payable in ready money six weeks after my death, 100

    And each year, from the date of my death, for her life, the interest of the above capital, 150

    After her death her son, Anton Polzelli, to receive 150 florins for one year, having always been a good son to his mother and a grateful pupil to me. *N.B.*—I hereby revoke the obligation in Italian, signed by me, which may be produced by Mdme. Polzelli, otherwise so many of my poor relations with greater claims would receive too little. Finally, Mdme. Polzelli must be satisfied with the annuity of 150 florins. After her death the half of the above capital, viz., 3000 florins, to be divided into two shares—one-half (1500) to devolve on the Rohrau family, for the purpose of keeping in good order the monument erected to me by Count von Harrach, and also that of my deceased father at the door of the sacristy. The other half to be held in trust by the Count, and the annual interest of the sum, namely, 45 florins, to be divided between any two orphans in Rohrau.
52. To my niece, Anna Lungmayer, payable six weeks after my death, 100

Likewise a yearly annuity to her husband and herself, 150
All these legacies and obligations, and also the proceeds of the sale
of my house and legal costs, to be paid within one year of my death;
all the other expenses to be deducted from the sum of ready money in
the hands of the executors, who must account to the heir for the same.
On their demise this annuity to go to their children until they come of
age, and after that period the capital to be equally divided among
them. Of the remaining 950 florins, 500 to become the property of
my beloved Count v. Harrach, as the depositary of my last will and
testament, and 300 I bequeath to the agent for his trouble. The resi-
due of 150 florins to go to my stepmother, and, if she be no longer
living, to her children. *N.B.*—Should Mdme. Lungmayer or her husband produce any document signed by me for a larger sum, I wish it
to be understood, as in the case of Mdme. Polzelli, that it is to be
considered null and void, as both Mdme. Lungmayer and her husband, owing to my great kindness, lavished more than 6000 florins of
mine during my life, which my own brother and the citizens in
Oedenberg and Eisenstadt can testify. (From No. 51 is repeatedly
and thickly scored out.)

53. To the widow Theresia Eder and her two daughters, lacemakers, 150
54. To my pupil, Anton Polzelli, 100
55. To poor blind Adam in Eisenstadt, 24
56. To my gracious Prince, my gold Parisian medal and the letter that
accompanied it, with a humble request to grant them a place in the
museum at Forchtentein.
57. To Mdlle. C. Czeck, waiting-woman to Princess Graschalkowitz
(erased), 1000
58. To Fräulein Anna Bucholz, 100
Inasmuch as in my youth her grandfather lent me 150 florins when
I greatly needed them, which, however, I repaid fifty years ago.
59. To the daughter of the bookkeeper, Kandler, my piano, by the organ-
builder Schanz.
60. The small Parisian medal to Count v. Harrach, and also the bust *d
l'antique* of Herr Grassi.
61. To the widow Wallnerin in Schottenhof, 100
62. To the Father Prior Leo in Eisenstadt, of the " Brothers of Mercy," 50
63. To the Hospital for the Poor in Eisenstadt (erased), 75

For the ratification of this my last will and testament, I have written it entirely in my own hand, and earnestly beg the authorities to consider it, even if not strictly or properly legal, in the light at least of a codicil, and to do all in their power to make it valid and binding.

JOSEPH HAYDN.

May 5, 1801.

Should God call me away suddenly, this my last will and testament, though not written on stamped paper, to be considered valid n law, and the stamps to be repaid tenfold to my sovereign.

In the name of the Holy Trinity. The uncertainty of the period when it may please my Creator, in His infinite wisdom, to call me from time into eternity has caused me, being in sound health, to make my last will with regard to my little remaining property. I commend my soul to my all-merciful Creator; my body I wish to be interred, according to the Roman Catholic forms, in consecrated ground. A first-class funeral. For my soul I bequeath No. 1.

JOSEPH HAYDN.

VIENNA, *Dec.* 6, 1801

Appendix B

CATALOGUE OF WORKS

THERE are unusual difficulties in the way of compiling a thoroughly satisfactory catalogue of Haydn's instrumental works. From the want of any generally-accepted consecutive numbering, and the fact that several are in the same key, this is particularly the case with the symphonies. Different editions have different numberings, and the confusion is increased by a further re-numbering of the piano symphonic scores arranged for two and four hands. In Breitkopf & Härtel's catalogue many works are included among the symphonies which are also found among the smaller compositions, and others are catalogued twice. Even the composer himself, in compiling his thematic catalogue, made mistakes. In the present list we have been content for the most part to state the numbers of the various instrumental works, without attempting to notify each individual composition. Indeed, to do otherwise would have called for an extensive use of music type. Nor have we thought it necessary to include the supposititious and doubtful works, for which Pohl's list may be consulted.

INSTRUMENTAL

125 symphonies, including overtures to operas and plays. Of these 94 are published in parts, 40 in score; 29 remain in MS. About 40 have been arranged for pianoforte 2 hands, 60 for 4 hands, 10 for 8 hands.

Pohl gives a thematic list of the 12 symphonies composed for Salomon, numbered in the order of their occurrence in the catalogue of the London Philharmonic Society. These include:

"The Surprise," G major, 1791
"The Clock," referring to the *Andante,* D minor, 1794
"The Military," G major, 1794

Other symphonies known by their titles are:

"Le Matin," D major
"Le Midi," C major
"Le Soir," G major, 1761
"The Farewell," A major, 1772
"Maria Theresa," C major, 1773
"The Schoolmaster," E flat, 1774
"Feuer Symphonie" (probably overture to "Die Feuersbrunst), A major
   1774
"La Chasse," D major, 1780
"Toy" Symphony, C major, 1780
"La Reine de France," B major, for Paris 1786
"The Oxford," G major, 1788
"The Seven Words from the Cross." Originally for orchestra. Arranged
   first for 2 violins, viola and bass; afterwards for soli, chorus and orchestra.
66 various compositions for wind and strings, separately and combined,
   including *divertimenti,* concerted pieces, etc.
7 notturnos or serenades for the lyre.
7 marches.
6 scherzandos.
1 sestet.
Several quintets.
1 "Echo" for 4 violins and 2 'cellos. "Feld-partien" for wind instruments and arrangements from baryton pieces.
12 collections of minuets and allemands.
31 concertos: 9 violin, 6 cello, 1 double bass, 5 lyre, 3 baryton, 2 flute,
   3 horn, 1 for 2 horns, 1 clarino (1796).
175 baryton pieces: Arrangements were published of several of these in
   3 parts, with violin (or flute), viola or cello as principal.
1 duet for 2 lutes.
2 trios for lute, violin and cello.
1 sonata for harp, with flute and bass.
Several pieces for a musical clock.
A solo for harmonica.
6 duets for violin solo, with viola accompaniments. The numerous printed
   duets for 2 violins are only arrangements from his other works.

30 trios: 20 for 2 violins and bass, 1 for violin solo, viola concertante and bass, 2 for flute, violin and bass, 3 for 3 flutes, 1 for corno di caccia, violin and cello.

77 quartets. The first 18 were published in 3 series; the next is in MS.; then i printed separately; 54 in 9 series of 6 Nos. each; 2 more and the last.

20 concertos and *divertimenti:* 1 concerto is with principal violin, 2 only (G and D) have been printed; the last alone survives.

38 trios: 35 with violin and cello, 3 with flute and cello Only 31 are printed.

53 sonatas and *divertimenti.* Only 35 are printed: the one in C, containing the adagio in F included in all the collections of smaller pieces, only in London.

4 sonatas for clavier and violin. 8 are published, but 4 of these are arrangements.

9 smaller pieces, including 5 Nos. of variations, a capriccio, a fantasia, 2 adagios and "différentes petites pièces."

1 duet (variations).

Church Music: 14 masses.

1 Stabat Mater.

2 Te Deums.

13 offertories. 10 of these are taken from other compositions with Latin text added.

4 motets.

1 Tantum Ergo.

4 Salve Reginas.

1 Regina Coeli.

2 Aves Reginas; Responsoria de Venerabili.

1 Cantilena pro Aventu (German words).

6 sacred arias.

2 duets.

"The Creation."

"The Seasons."

" II Ritorno di Tobia."
"The Seven Words."
" Invocation of Neptune."
"Applausus Musicus." For the festival of a prelate, 1768.
Cantata for the birthday of Prince Nicolaus, 1763.
Cantata " Die Erwählung eines Kapellmeisters."

OPERAS

Italian Operas: "La Canterina," 1769; "L'Incontro Improvise," 1776; "Lo Speciale," 1768; "Le Pescatrice," 1780; "II Mondo della Luna," 1877; "L'Isola Disabitata," 1779; "Armida," 1782: "L'Infedeltà Delusa," 1773; "La Fedeltà Premiata," 1780; "La Vera Constanza," 1786; "Acide e Galatea," 1762; "Orlando Paladino," 1782; "Orfeo," London, 1794.

German Opera or Singspiel: "Der Neue Krumme Teufel."
5 marionette operas.
Music for "Alfred," a tragedy, and various other plays.

MISCELLANEOUS

SONGS: 12 German lieder, 1782; 12 ditto, 1784; 12 single songs; 6 original canzonets, London, 1796; 6 ditto; "The Spirit Song," Shakespeare (F minor); "O Tuneful Voice" (E flat), composed for an English lady of position; 3 English songs in MS.; 2 duets; 3 three-part and 10 four-part songs; 3 choruses, MS.; 1 ditto from "Alfred;" The Austrian National Anthem, for single voice and in 4 parts; 42 canons in 2 and more parts; 2 ditto; "The Ten Commandments" set to canons; the same with different words under the title "Die zehn Gesetze der Kunst"; symphonies and accompaniments for national songs in the collections of Whyte, Napier and George Thomson.

22 airs mostly inserted in operas.
"Ariana a Naxos," cantata for single voice and pianoforte, 1790.
"Deutschlands Klage auf den Tod Friedrichs der Grossen," cantata for single voice, with baryton accompaniment, 1787.

Appendix C

BIBLIOGRAPHY

THE Haydn literature is almost entirely Continental. With the exceptions of Pohl's article in Grove's "Dictionary of Music" and Miss Townsend's "Haydn," nothing of real importance has appeared in English. The following list does not profess to be complete. It seems futile in a book of this kind to refer amateurs and students to foreign works, many of which are out of print and others generally inaccessible. For the benefit of English readers the English works have been placed first and apart from the Continental. It has not been thought necessary to follow Pohl in giving a separate list of German and other Continental *critiques*. His plan of citing works in the order of their publication has, however, been adopted as being perhaps preferable to an alphabetical order of writers.

"History of Music," Vol. IV. Burney London, 1789

"Reminiscences," Vol. I., p. 190, Michael Kelly, London, 1826

"Musical Memoirs," Parke, London, 1830, 2 vols.

"Letters of Distinguished Musicians." Translated from the German by Lady Wallace. Haydn's Letters, pp. 71-204, with portrait, London, 1867

"Musical Composers and their Works"—Haydn, pp. 57-75, Sarah Tytler, London, 1875

"Music and Morals"—Haydn, pp. 241-263, Haweis, London, 1876

Leisure Hour, p. 572. Article, "Anecdotes of Haydn, " London, 1877

"The Great Composers Sketched by Themselves"—No. 1, Haydn. An estimate of Haydn drawn mainly from his letters, Joseph Bennett, *London Musical Times*, London, Sept. 1877

Article on Haydn in Grove's "Dictionary of Music," Pohl, London 1879

"Studies of Great Composers,"—Haydn, pp. 91-118, with portrait, Parry, London, 1887

"History of Music," English edition, Vol. IV., pp. 852-882. Portraits and facsimiles, Naumann, London (Cassell), 1888

"Musical Reminiscences"—*Music and Sunshine*, pp. 141-149, with quotations from Haydn's music to show "the happy state of his mind whilst composing," William Spark, London, 1892

"Musical Haunts in London"—Haydn in London, pp. 32-36, F. G. Edwards, London 1895

"The Pianoforte Sonata"— J. S. Shedlock, London 1895

"Music and Manners from Pergolese to Beethoven"— Haydn in London: (1) His Note-book; (2) His English Love, pp. 57-95, Krehbiel, London, 1898

"George Thomson, the Friend of Burns"—Correspondence with Haydn, pp. 303-308, Cuthbert Hadden, London 1898

"Old Scores and New Readings"—Haydn and his "Creation," pp. 85-92, J. F. Runciman, London 1899

"The Birthplace of Haydn: a Visit to Rohrau" Dr. Frank Merrick, London Musical Times, July 1899

"Joseph Haydn" in Great Musicians series, Miss Pauline D. Townsend, London, n.d.

Article on Haydn in "Dictionary of Music." English ed. translated by
J. S. Shedlock; Riemann, London, Augener and Co.

Autobiographical Sketch by himself. This was made use of by (1) De
Luca in "Das gelehrte Oesterreich," 1778; (2) In Forkel's "musickalischer
Almanach für Deutschland," 1783; and (3) in the *European Magazine*
for October 1784. The latter includes a portrait, 1776

"Lexicon," Additional particulars are given in 2nd edition, 1812, Gerber,
1790
Musik Correspondenz der deutschen Filarm. *Gesselschaft*, Nos. 17
and 18, Gerber, 1792

Article in *Journal des Luxus und der Moden*, Bertuch, Weimar, 1805

"Brevi notizie istorchie della vita e delle opere di Guis. Haydn," Mayer,
Bergamo, 1809

Obituary in the *Vaterländ. Blätter für den öst Kaiserstaat*, Vienna,
1809

"Der Nagedachtenis van J. Haydn," Kinker, Amsterdam, 1810

Biographische Notizen über Joseph Haydn," Griezinger, Leipzig, 1810

"Biographische Nachrichten von Joseph Haydn," Dies, Vienna, 1810

"Joseph Haydn," Arnold, Erfurt, 1810; 2nd ed. 1825

"Notice sur J. Haydn" Framery, Paris, 1810

"Notice historique sur la vie et les ouvrages de Haydn" in the *Moniteur.*
This was reprinted in the "Bibliographie Musicale," Paris, 1822. It was
also translated into Portuguese, with additions by Silva-Lisboa. Rio Ja-
neiro, 1820; Le Breton, Paris, 1810

"Essai Historique sur la vie de J.Haydn," Strassburg, 1812

" Le Haydine," etc. This work was essentially reproduced, 2nd edition, without acknowledgment, in "Lettres écrites de Vienne en Autriche," etc., by L. A. C. Bombet, Paris, 1814; re-published as "Vie de Haydn, Mozart et Metastase," par Stendhal, Paris, 1817. Bombet and Stendhal are both pseudonyms of Henri Beyle. An English translation of the 1814 work was published in London by John Murray, in 1817, under the title of " The Life of Haydn in a Series of Letters," etc. *See* p. 76 of text. Carpani Milan, 1812; 2nd edition enlarged, Padua, 1823

"Biogr. Notizen," Grosser, Hirschberg, 1826

" Allg. Encyclopädie der Wissenschaften und Künste," 2nd section, 3rd part, with a biographical sketch by Fröhlich, Ersch und Gruber, Leipzig, 1828

" Allg. Wiener Musikzeitung," 1843

"J. Haydn in London, 1791 and 1792," Karajan Vienna, 1861

"Joseph Haydn und sein Bruder Michael," Wurzbach, Vienna, 1861

"Joseph Haydn," Ludwig, Nordhausen, 1867

" Mozart and Haydn in London," Pohl, Vienna, 1867

"Joseph Haydn." This, the first comprehensive biography of Haydn, was published—the first half of Vol. I. in 1875, the second half in 1882. After the death of Pohl in 1887 it was completed (1890) by E. V. Mandyczewski, Pohl.

Notice in "Biographie Universelle," Fétis.

Appendix D

HAYDN'S BROTHERS

OF the large family born to the Rohrau wheelright, two, besides the great composer, devoted themselves to music.

The first, JOHANN EVANGELIST HAYDN, made some little reputation as a vocalist, and was engaged in that capacity in the Esterhazy Chapel. His health had, however, been delicate from the first, and his professional career was far from prosperous.

JOHANN MICHAEL HAYDN was much more distinguished. Born in 1737, he became, as we have seen, a chorister and solo-vocalist at St Stephen's, Vienna. He was a good violinist, and played the organ so well that he was soon able to act as deputy-organist at the cathedral. In 1757 he was appointed Capellmeister to the Bishop of Grosswardein, and in 1762 became conductor, and subsequently leader and organist to Archbishop Sigismund of Salzburg. There he naturally came in contact with Mozart, in whose biography his name is often mentioned. Mozart on one occasion wrote two compositions for him which the archbishop received as Michael Haydn's. The Concertmeister was incapacitated by illness at the time, and Mozart came to his rescue to save his salary, which the archbishop had characteristically threatened to stop. Mozart also scored several of his sacred works for practice.

Michael Haydn remained at Salzburg till his death in 1806. He had the very modest salary of £24, with board and lodging, which was afterwards doubled; but although he was more than once offered preferment elsewhere, he declined to leave his beloved Salzburg. He was happily married—in 1768—to a daughter of Lipp, the cathedral organist; and with his church work, his pupils—among whom were Reicha and Weber—and his compositions, he sought nothing more. When the French entered Salzburg and pillaged the city in 1801 he was among the victims, losing some property and a month's salary, but his brother and friends repaired the loss with interest. This misfortune led the Empress Maria Theresa to commission him to compose a mass, for which she rewarded him munificently. Another of his masses was written for Prince Esterhazy, who twice offered him the vice-Capellmeistership of the chapel at Eisenstadt. Joseph thought Michael too straightforward for this post. "Ours is a court life," he said, "but a very different one from yours at Salzburg. It is uncommonly hard to do what you want." If any appointment could have drawn him away from Salzburg it was this; and it is said that he refused it only because he hoped that the chapel at Salzburg would be reorganised and his salary raised.

Michael Haydn is buried in a side chapel of St Peter's Church, Salzburg. A monument was erected in 1821, and over it is an urn containing his skull. He is described by Pohl as "upright, good-tempered and modest; a little rough in manners, and in later life given to drink." His correspondence shows him to have been a warm-hearted friend; and he had the same devout practice of initialling his manuscripts as his brother. The latter thought highly of him as a composer, declaring that his Church compositions were superior to his own in earnestness, severity of style and sustained power. When he asked leave to copy the canons which hung in Joseph's bedroom at Vienna, Joseph replied: "Get away with your copies; you can compose much better for yourself." Michael's statement has often been quoted: "Give me good librettos and the same patronage as my brother, and I should not be behind him." This could scarcely have been the case, since, as Pohl points out, Michael Haydn failed in the very qualities which ensured his brother's success. As it was, he wrote a very large number of works, most of which remained in manuscript. A Mass in D is his best-known composition, though mention should be made of the popular common-metre tune "Salzburg," adapted from a mass composed for the use of country choirs. Michael Haydn was nominated the great composer's sole heir, but his death frustrated the generous intention.

Appendix E

A SELECTION OF HAYDN LETTERS

THE greater number of Haydn's extant letters deal almost exclusively with business matters, and are therefore of comparatively little interest to the reader of his life. The following selection may be taken as representing the composer in his more personal and social relations. It is drawn from the correspondence with Frau von Genzinger, which was discovered by Theodor Georg von Karajan, in Vienna, and published first in the *Jahrbuch für Vaterländische Geschichte,* and afterwards in his *J. Haydn in London,* 1791 and 1792 (1861). The translation here used, by the courtesy of Messrs Longman, is that of Lady Wallace.

The name of Frau von Genzinger has been mentioned more than once in the biography. Her husband was the Esterhazy physician. In that capacity he paid frequent visits to Eisenstadt and Esterhaz (which Haydn spells Estoras) and so became intimate with the Capellmeister. He was fond of music, and during the long winter evenings in Vienna was in the habit of assembling the best artists in his house at Schottenhof, where on Sundays Mozart, Haydn, Dittersdorf, Albrechtsberger, and others were often to be found. His wife, Marianne—*née* von Kayser—was a good singer, and was sought after by all the musical circles in Vienna. She was naturally attracted to Haydn, and although she was nearly forty years of age when the correspondence opened in 1789, "a personal connection was gradually developed in the course of their musical intercourse that eventually touched their hearts and gave rise to a bright bond of friendship between the lady and the old, though still youthful, *maestro.*" Some brief extracts from the letters now to be given have of necessity been worked into the biography. The correspondence originated in the following note from Frau von Genzinger:

January 1789.

DEAR M. HAYDN—With your kind permission I take the liberty to send a pianoforte arrangement of the beautiful *adagio* in your admirable com-

131

position. 1 arranged it from the score quite alone, and without the least help from my master. I beg that, if you should discover any errors, you will be so good as to correct them. I do hope that you are in perfect health, and nothing do I wish more than to see you soon again in Vienna, in order to prove further my high esteem.—Your obedient servant,

MARIA ANNA V. GENZINGER.

To this Haydn replies as follows:

ESTORAS, *Janr.* 14, 1789.

DEAR MADAM—In all my previous correspondence, nothing was ever so agreeable to me as the surprise of seeing your charming writing, and reading so many kind expressions; but still more did I admire what you sent me—the admirable arrangement of the *adagio,* which, from its correctness, might be engraved at once by any publisher. I should like to know whether you arranged the *adagio* from the score, or whether you gave yourself the amazing trouble of first putting it into score from the separate parts, and then arranging it for the piano, for, if the latter, such an attention would be too flattering to me, and I feel that I really do not deserve it.

Best and kindest Frau v. Genzinger! I only await a hint from you as to how, and in what way, I can serve you; in the meantime, I return the *adagio,* and hope that my talents, poor though they be, may ensure me some commands from you.—I am yours, etc.,

HAYDN.

The next letter is from the lady:

VIENNA, *Oct.*29, 1789.

DEAR HERR V. HAYDN—I hope you duly received my letter of September 15, and also the first movement of the symphony 204 (the *andante* of which I sent you some months ago), and now follows the last movement, which I have arranged for the piano as well as it was in my power to do; I only wish that it may please you, and earnestly beg that, if there are any mistakes in it, you will correct them at your leisure, a service which I shall always accept from you, my valued Herr Haydn, with the utmost gratitude. Be so good as to let me know whether you received my letter of September 15, and the piece of music, and if it is in accordance with your taste, which would delight me very much, for I am very uneasy and concerned lest you should not have got it safely, or not approve of it. I hope that you are well, which will always be a source of pleasure to me to hear, and commending myself to your further friendship and remembrance.—I remain, your devoted friend and servant,

MARIA ANNA V. GENZINGER., née V. KAYSER.

My husband sends you his regards.

To Frau v. Genzinger.

Nov. 9, 1789.

DEAR MADAM—I beg your forgiveness a million times for having so long delayed returning your laborious and admirable work: the last time my apartments were cleared out, which occurred just after receiving your first movement, it was mislaid by my copyist among the mass of my other music, and only a few days ago I had the good fortune to find it in an old opera score.

Dearest and kindest Frau v. Genzinger! do not be displeased with a man who values you so highly; I should be inconsolable if by the delay I were to lose any of your favour, of which I am so proud.

These two pieces are arranged quite as correctly as the first. I cannot but admire the trouble and the patience you lavish on my poor talents; and allow me to assure you in return that, in my frequent evil moods, nothing cheers me so much as the flattering conviction that I am kindly remembered by you; for which favour I kiss your hands a thousand times, and am, with sincere esteem, your obedient servant,

JOSEPH HAYDN.

P.S.—I shall soon claim permission to wait on you.

The next letter is again from Frau v. Genzinger;

VIENNA, *Nov.* 12, 1789.

MY VALUED HERR V. HAYDN—I really cannot tell you all the pleasure I felt in reading your highly-prized letter of the 9th. How well am I rewarded for my trouble by seeing your satisfaction! Nothing do I wish more ardently than to have more time (now so absorbed by household affairs), for in that case I would certainly devote many hours to music, my most agreeable and favourite of all occupations. You must not, my dear Herr v. Haydn, take it amiss that I plague you with another letter, but I could not but take advantage of so good an opportunity to inform you of the safe arrival of your letter. I look forward with the utmost pleasure to the happy day when I am to see you in Vienna. Pray continue to give me a place in your friendship and remembrance.—Your sincere and devoted friend and servant.

To Frau v. Genzinger.

ESTORAS, *Nov.* 18,1789.

DEAR LADY—The letter which I received through Herr Siebert gave me another proof of your excellent heart, as instead of a rebuke for my late remissness, you express yourself in so friendly a manner towards me, that so much indulgence, kindness and great courtesy cause me the utmost surprise, and I kiss your hands in return a thousand times. If my poor talents enable me to respond in any degree to so much that is nattering, I venture, dear madam, to offer you a little musical *potpourri.* I do not, indeed, find in it much that is fragrant; perhaps the publisher may rectify the fault in future editions. If the arrangement of the symphony in it be yours, oh! then I shall be twice as much pleased with the publisher; if not, I venture to ask you to arrange a symphony, and to transcribe it with your own hand, and to send it to me here, when I will at once forward it to my publisher at Leipzig to be engraved.

I am happy to have found an opportunity that leads me to hope for a few more charming lines from you.—I am, etc.,

JOSEPH HAYDN.

Shortly after the date of this letter Hadyn was again in Vienna, when the musical evenings at Schottenhof were renewed. The Herr v. Häring referred to in the following note is doubtless the musical banker, well known as a violinist in the Vienna of the time.

To Frau v. Genzinger.

Jan. 23,1790.

DEAR, KIND FRAU V. GENZINGER—I beg to inform you that all arrangements are now completed for the little quartet party that we agreed to have next Friday. Herr v. Häring esteemed himself very fortunate in being able to be of use to me on this occasion, and the more so when I told him of all the attention I had received from you, and your other merits.

What I care about is a little approval. Pray don't forget to invite the Pater Professor. Meanwhile, I kiss your hands, and am, with profound respect, yours, etc.,

HAYDN.

A call to return to Esterhaz put an end to these delights of personal intercourse, as will be gathered from the following letter:

To Frau v. Genzinger.

Feb. 3, 1790.

NOBLEST AND KINDEST LADY—However nattering the last invitation you gave me yesterday to spend this evening with you, I feel with deep regret that I am even unable to express to you personally my sincere thanks for all your past kindness. Bitterly as I deplore this, with equal truth do I fervently wish you, not only on this evening, but ever and always, the most agreeable social "reunions"—mine are all over—and to-morrow I return to dreary solitude! May God only grant me health; but I fear the contrary, being far from well to-day. May the Almighty preserve you, dear lady, and your worthy husband, and all your beautiful children. Once more I kiss your hands, and am unchangeably while life lasts, yours, etc.,

HAYDN.

The next letter was written six days later, evidently in the most doleful mood:

To Frau v. Genzinger.

ESTORAS, *Feb.* 9, 1790.

MUCH ESTEEMED AND KINDEST FRAU V. GENZINGER— Well! here I sit in my wilderness; forsaken, like some poor orphan, almost without human society; melancholy, dwelling on the memory of past glorious days. Yes; past, alas! And who can tell when these happy hours may return? those charming meetings? where the whole circle have but one heart and one soul—all those delightful musical evenings, which can only be remembered, and not described. Where are all those inspired moments? All gone—and gone for long. You must not be surprised, dear lady, that I have delayed writing to express my gratitude. I found everything at home in confusion; for three days I did not know whether I was *capell* master, or *capell* servant; nothing could console me; my apartments were all in confusion; my pianoforte, that I formerly loved so dearly, was perverse and disobedient, and rather irritated than soothed me. I slept very little, and even my dreams persecuted me, for, while asleep, I was under the pleasant delusion that I was listening to the opera of "Le Nozze di Figaro," when the blustering north wind woke me, and almost blew my nightcap off my head.

. . . Forgive me,[30] dear lady, for taking up your time in this very first letter by so wretched a scrawl, and such stupid nonsense; you must forgive a man spoilt by the Viennese. Now, however, I begin to accustom myself by degrees to country life, and yesterday I studied for the first time, and somewhat in the Haydn style too.

No doubt, you have been more industrious than myself. The pleasing *adagio* from the quartet has probably now received its true expression from your fair fingers. I trust that my good Fräulein Peperl[31] may be frequently reminded of her master, by often singing over the cantata, and that she will pay particular attention to distinct articulation and correct vocalisation, for it would be a sin if so fine a voice were to remain imprisoned in the breast. I beg, therefore, for a frequent smile, or else I shall be much vexed. I advise M. François[32] too to cultivate his musical talents. Even if he sings in his dressing-gown, it will do well enough, and I will often write something new to encourage him. I again kiss your hands in gratitude for all the kindness you have shown me. I am, etc.,

HAYDN.

To Frau v. Gensinger.

ESTORAS, *March* 14, 1790.

MOST VALUED, ESTEEMED AND KINDEST FRAU V. GENZINGER—I ask forgiveness a million times for having so long delayed answering your two charming letters, which has not been caused by negligence (a sin from which may Heaven preserve me so long as I live), but from the press of business which has devolved on me for my gracious Prince, in his present melancholy condition. The death of his wife overwhelmed the Prince with such grief that we were obliged to use every means in our power to rouse him from his profound sorrow. I therefore arranged for the three first days a selection of chamber music, but no singing. The poor Prince, however, the first evening, on hearing my favourite *Adagio* in D, was affected by such deep melancholy that it was difficult to disperse it by other pieces. On the fourth day we had an opera, the fifth a comedy, and then our theatre daily as usual. . .

You must now permit me to kiss your hands gratefully for the rusks you sent me, which, however, I did not receive till last Tuesday; but they came exactly at the right moment, having just finished the last of the others. That my favourite "Ariadne" has been successful at Schottenhof is delightful news to me, but I recommend Fräulein Peperl to articulate the words clearly, especially in the words "Che tanto amai." I also take the liberty of wishing you all possible good on your approaching nameday, begging you to continue your favour towards me, and to consider me on every occasion as your own, though unworthy, master. I must also mention that the teacher of languages can come here any day, and his journey will be paid. He can travel either by the diligence or by some other conveyance, which can always be heard of in the Madschaker Hot. As I feel sure, dear lady, that you take an interest in all that concerns me (far greater than I deserve), I must inform you that last week I received a present of a handsome gold snuff-box, the weight of thirty-four ducats, from Prince Oetting v. Wallerstein, accompanied by an invitation to pay him a visit this year, the Prince defraying my expenses, His Highness being desirous to make my personal acquaintance (a pleasing fillip to my depressed spirits). Whether I shall make up my mind to the journey is another question. I beg you will excuse this hasty scrawl—I am always, etc.,

HAYDN.

P.S.—I have just lost my faithful coachman; he died on the 25th of last month.

To Frau v. Genzinger.

ESTORAS, *May* 13, 1790.

BEST AND KINDEST FRAU V. GENZINGER— I was quite surprised, on receiving your esteemed letter, to find that you had not yet got my last letter, in which I mentioned that our landlord had accepted the services of a French teacher, who came by chance to Estoras, and I also made my excuses both to you and your tutor on that account. My highly esteemed benefactress, this is not the first time that some of my letters and of others also have been lost, inasmuch as our letter bag, on its way to Oedenburg (in order to have letters put into it), is always opened by the steward there, which has frequently been the cause of mistake and other disagreeable occurrences. For greater security, however, and to defeat such disgraceful curiosity, I will henceforth enclose all my letters in a separate envelope to the porter, Herr Pointer. This trick annoys me the more because you might justly reproach me with procrastination, from which may Heaven defend me! At all events, the prying person, whether male or female, cannot, either in this last letter or in any of the others, have discovered anything in the least inconsistent with propriety. And now, my esteemed patroness, when am I to have the inexpressible happiness of seeing you in Estoras? As business does not admit of my going to Vienna, I console myself by the hope of kissing your hands here this summer. In which pleasing hope, I am, with high consideration, etc., yours,

HAYDN.

To Frau v. Genzinger.

ESTORAS, *May* 30, 1790.

KINDEST AND BEST FRAU V. GENZINGER—I was at Oedenburg when I received your last welcome letter, having gone there on purpose to enquire about the lost letter. The steward there vowed by all that was holy that he had seen no letter at that time in my writing, so that it must have been lost in Estoras! Be this as it may, such curiosity can do me no harm, far less yourself, as the whole contents of the letter were an account of my opera "La Vera Costanza," performed in the new theatre in the Landstrasse, and about the French teacher who was to have come at that time to Estoras. You need, therefore, be under no uneasiness, dear lady, either as regards the past or the future, for my friendship and esteem for you (tender as they are) can never become reprehensible, having always before my eyes respect for your elevated virtues, which not only I, but all who know you, must reverence. Do not let this deter you from consoling me sometimes by your agreeable letters, as they are so highly necessary to cheer me in this wilderness, and to soothe my deeply wounded heart. Oh! that I could be with you, dear lady, even for one quarter of an hour, to pour forth all my sorrows, and to receive comfort from you. I am obliged to submit to many vexations from our official managers here, which, however, I shall at present pass over in silence. The sole consolation left me is that I am, thank God, well, and eagerly disposed to work. I only regret that, with this inclination, you have waited so long for the promised symphony. On this occasion it really proceeds from absolute necessity, arising from my circumstances, and the raised prices of everything. I trust, therefore, that you will not be displeased with your Haydn, who, often as his Prince absents himself from Estoras, never can obtain leave, even for four-and-twenty hours, to go to Vienna. It is scarcely credible, and yet the refusal is always couched in such polite terms, and in such a manner, as to render it utterly impossible for me to urge my request for leave of absence. Well, as God pleases! This time also will pass away, and the day return when I shall again have the inexpressible pleasure of being seated beside you at the pianoforte, hearing Mozart's masterpieces, and kissing your hands from gratitude for so much pleasure. With this hope, I am, etc.,

J. HAYDN.

To Frau v. Genzinger.

ESTORAS, June 6, 1790.

DEAR AND ESTEEMED LADY—I heartily regret that you were so long in receiving my last letter. But the previous week no messenger was despatched from Estoras, so it was not my fault that the letter reached you so late. *Between ourselves!* I must inform you that Mademoiselle Nanette has commissioned me to compose a new sonata for you, to be given into your hands alone. I esteem myself fortunate in having received such a command. You will receive the sonata in a fortnight at latest. Mademoiselle Nanette promised me payment for the work, but you can easily imagine that on no account would I accept it. For me the best reward will always be to hear that I have in some degree met with your approval. I am, etc.,

HAYDN.

To Frau v. Genzinger.

ESTORAS, June 20, 1790.

DEAR, KIND FRIEND—I take the liberty of sending you a new pianoforte sonata with violin or flute, not as anything at all remarkable, but as a trifling resource in case of any great *ennui.* I only beg that you will have it copied out as soon as possible, and then return it to me. The day before yesterday I presented to Mademoiselle Nanette the sonata commanded by her. I had hoped she would express a wish to hear me play it, but I have not yet received any order to that effect; I, therefore, do not know whether you will receive it by this post or not. The sonata is in E flat, newly written, and always intended for you. It is strange enough that the final movement of this sonata contains the very same minuet and trio that you asked me for in your last letter. This identical work was destined for you last year, and I have only written a new *adagio* since then, which I strongly recommend to your attention. It has a deep signification which I will analyse for you when opportunity offers. It is rather difficult, but full of feeling. What a pity that you have not one of Schanz's pianos, for then you could produce twice the effect!

N.B.—Mademoiselle Nanette must know nothing of the sonata being already half written before I received her commands, for this might suggest notions with regard to me that I might find most prejudicial, and I must be very careful not to lose her favour. In the meanwhile I consider myself fortunate to be the means of giving her pleasure, particularly as the sacrifice is made for your sake, my charming Frau v. Genzinger. Oh! how I do wish that I could only play over these sonatas once or twice to you; how gladly would I then reconcile myself to remain for a time in my wilderness! I have much to say and to confess to you, from which no one but yourself can absolve me; but what cannot be effected now will, I devoutly hope, come to pass next winter, and half of the time is already gone. Meanwhile I take refuge in patience, and am content with the inestimable privilege of subscribing myself your sincere and obedient friend and servant,

J. HAYDN.

To Frau v. Genzinger.

ESTORAS, June 27, 1790.

HIGHLY ESTEEMED LADY—You have no doubt by this time received the new pianoforte sonata, and, if not, you will probably do so along with this letter. Three days ago I played the sonata to Mademoiselle Nanette in the presence of my gracious Prince. At first I doubted very much, owing to its difficulty, whether I should receive any applause, but was soon convinced of the reverse by a gold snuff-box being presented to me by Mademoiselle Nanette's own hand. My sole wish now is, that you may be satisfied with it, so that I may find greater credit with my patroness. For the same reason, I beg that either you or your husband will let her know "that my delight was such that I could not conceal her generosity," especially being convinced that you take an interest in all benefits conferred on me. It is a pity that you have not a Schanz pianoforte, which is much more favourable to expression; my idea is that you should make over your own still very tolerable piano to Fräulein Peperl, and get a new one for yourself. Your beautiful hands, and their brilliant execution, deserve this, and more. I know that I ought to have composed the sonata in accordance with the capabilities of your piano, but, being so unaccustomed to this, I found it impossible, and now I am doomed to stay at home. What I lose by so doing you can well imagine: it is indeed sad always to be a slave—but Providence wills it so. I am a poor creature, plagued perpetually by hard work, and with few hours for recreation. Friends? What do I say? *One* true friend; there are no longer any true friends, but one female friend. Oh yes! no doubt I still have one, but she is far away. Ah well! I take refuge in my thoughts. May God bless her, and may she never forget me! Meanwhile I kiss your hands a thousand times, and ever am, etc.,

HAYDN.

Pray forgive my bad writing. I am suffering from inflamed eyes to-day.

To Frau v. Genzinger.

ESTORAS, *July* 4, 1790.

MOST ESTEEMED AND VALUED LADY—I this moment receive your letter, and at the same time the post departs. I sincerely rejoice to hear that my Prince intends to present you with a new piano, more especially as I am in some measure the cause of this, having been constantly imploring Mademoiselle Nanette to persuade your husband to purchase one for you. The choice now depends entirely on yourself, and the chief point is that you should select one in accordance with your touch and your taste. Certainly my friend, Herr Walter, is very celebrated, and every year I receive the greatest civility from him; but, *entre nous,* and to speak candidly, sometimes there is not more than one out of ten of his instruments which may be called really good, and they are exceedingly high priced besides. I know Herr Nickl's piano; it is first-rate, but too heavy for your touch; nor can every passage be rendered with proper delicacy on it. I should, therefore, like you to try one of Herr Schanz's pianos, for they have a remarkably light and agreeable touch. A good pianoforte is absolutely necessary for you, and my sonata will also gain vastly by it.

Meanwhile I thank you much, dear lady, for your caution with regard to Mademoiselle Nanette. It is a pity that the little gold box she gave me, and had used herself, is tarnished, but perhaps I may get it polished up in Vienna. I have as yet received no orders to purchase a pianoforte. I fear that one may be sent to your house, which may be handsome outside, but the touch within heavy. If your husband will rely on my opinion, that

Herr Schanz is the best maker for this class of instruments, I would then settle everything at once. In great haste, yours, etc.,

HAYDN.

To Frau v. Genzinger.

ESTORAS, *August* 15.

I ought to have written to you last week in answer to your letter, but as this day has been long enshrined in my heart, I have been striving earnestly all the time to think how and what I was to wish for you; so thus eight days passed, and now, when my wishes ought to be expressed, my small amount of intellect comes to a standstill, and (quite abashed) I find nothing to say; why? wherefore? because I have not been able to fulfil those musical hopes for this particular day that you have justly the right to expect. Oh, my most charming and kind benefactress! if you could only know, or see into my troubled heart on this subject, you would certainly feel pity and indulgence for me. The unlucky promised symphony has haunted my imagination ever since it was bespoken, and it is only, alas! the pressure of urgent occurrences that has prevented its being hitherto ushered into the world! The hope, however, of your lenity towards me for the delay, and the approaching time of the fulfilment of my promise, embolden me to express my wish, which, among the hundreds offered to you to-day and yesterday, may perhaps appear to you only an insignificant interloper; I say *perhaps,* for it would be too bold in me to think that you could form no better wish for yourself than mine. You see, therefore, most kind and charming lady, that I can wish nothing for you on your nameday, because my wishes are too feeble, and therefore unproductive. As for me, I venture to wish for myself your kind indulgence, and the continuance of your friendship, and the goodness that I so highly prize. This is my warmest wish! But if any wish of mine may be permitted, then mine shall become identical with your own, for thus I shall feel assured that none other remains, except the wish once more to be allowed to subscribe myself your very sincere friend and servant,

HAYDN.

No further letters appear to have been addressed to the lady until Haydn started on his first visit to London in December 1790. One or two extracts from these London letters have been used in Chapter V., but as the repetitions will be very slight, we allow the letters to stand as they are.

To Frau v. Genzinger.

CALAIS, *Dec.* 31, 1790.

HIGHLY HONOURED LADY—A violent storm and an incessant pour of rain prevented our arriving at Calais till this evening (where I am now writing to you), and to-morrow at seven in the morning we cross the sea to London. I promised to write from Brussels, but we could only stay there an hour. I am very well, thank God! although somewhat thinner, owing to fatigue, irregular sleep, and eating and drinking so many different things. A few days hence I will describe the rest of my journey, but I must beg you to excuse me for to-day. I hope to heaven that you and your husband and children are all well. —I am, with high esteem, etc., yours,

HAYDN.

To Frau v. Genzinger.

LONDON, *Jan.* 8, 1791.

I thought that you had received my last letter from Calais. I ought, indeed, according to my promise, to have sent you some tidings of myself when I arrived in London, but I preferred waiting a few days that I might detail various incidents to you. I must now tell you that on New Year's Day, after attending early mass, I took ship at half-past seven o'clock a.m., and at five o'clock in the afternoon arrived safe and well at Dover, for which Heaven be praised! During the first four hours there was scarcely any wind, and the vessel made so little way that in that time we only went one English mile, there being twenty-four between Calais and Dover. The ship's captain, in the worst possible humour, said that if the wind did not change we should be at sea all night. Fortunately, however, towards half-past eleven o'clock such a favourable breeze began to blow that by four o'clock we had come twenty-two miles. As the ebb of the tide prevented our large vessel making the pier, two small boats were rowed out to meet us, into which we and our luggage were transferred, and at last we landed safely, though exposed to a sharp gale. The large vessel stood out to sea five hours longer, till the tide carried it into harbour. Some of the passengers, being afraid to trust themselves in the small boats, stayed on board, but I followed the example of the greater number. I remained on deck during the whole passage, in order to gaze my fill at that huge monster, the Ocean. So long as there was a calm I had no fears, but when at length a violent wind began to blow, rising every minute, and I saw the boisterous high waves running on, I was seized with a little alarm, and a little indisposition likewise. But I overcame it all, and arrived safely in harbour, without being actually ill. Most of the passengers were ill, and looked like ghosts. I did not feel the fatigue of the journey till I arrived in London, but it took two days before I could recover from it. But now I am quite fresh and well, and occupied in looking at this mighty and vast town of London, its various beauties and marvels causing me the most profound astonishment. I immediately paid the necessary visits, such as to the Neapolitan Minister and to our own. Both called on me in return two days afterwards, and a few days ago I dined with the former—*nota bene,* at six o'clock in the evening, which is the fashion here.

My arrival caused a great sensation through the whole city, and I went the round of all the newspapers for three successive days. Everyone seems anxious to know me. I have already dined out six times, and could be invited every day if I chose; but I must in the first place consider my health, and in the next my work. Except the nobility, I admit no visitors till two o'clock in the afternoon, and at four o'clock I dine at home with Salomon. I have a neat, comfortable lodging, but very dear. My landlord is an Italian, and likewise a cook, who gives us four excellent dishes; we each pay one florin thirty kreuzers a day, exclusive of wine and beer, but everything is terribly dear here. I was yesterday invited to a grand amateur concert, but as I arrived rather late, when I gave my ticket, they would not let me in, but took me to an ante-room, where I was obliged to remain till the piece which was then being given was over. Then they opened the door, and I was conducted, leaning on the arm of the director, up the centre of the room to the front of the orchestra amid universal clapping of hands, stared at by everyone, and greeted by a number of English compliments. I was assured that such honours had not been conferred on anyone for fifty years. After the concert I was taken into a very handsome room adjoining, where tables were laid for all the amateurs, to the number of two hundred. It was proposed that I should take a seat near the top, but as it so happened that I had dined out that very day, and ate more than usual, I declined the honour, excusing myself under the pretext of not being very well; but in spite of this, I could not get off drinking the health, in Burgundy, of the harmonious gentlemen present; all responded to it, but at last allowed me to go home. All this, my dear lady, was very flattering to me; still I wish I could fly for a time to Vienna, to have more peace to work, for the noise in the streets, and the cries of the common people selling their wares, is intolerable. I am still working at symphonies, as the libretto of the opera is not yet decided on, but in order to be more quiet, I intend to engage an apartment some little way out of town. I would gladly write more at length, but I fear losing this opportunity. With kindest regards to your husband, Fräulein Pepi, and all the rest, I am, with sincere esteem, etc.,

HAYDN.

P.S.—I have a request to make. I think I must have left my symphony in E flat, that you returned to me, in my room at home, or mislaid it on the journey. I missed it yesterday, and being in pressing need of it, I beg you urgently to procure it for me, through my kind friend, Herr v. Kees. Pray have it copied out in your own house, and send it by post as soon as possible. If Herr v. Kees hesitates about this, which I don't think likely, pray send him this letter. My address is, M. Haydn, 18 Great Pulteney Street, London.

To Frau v. Genzinger.

LONDON, *Sept.* 17, 1791.

MY HIGHLY ESTEEMED FRIEND—I have received no reply to my two let-ters of July 3, entrusted to the care of a composer, Herr Diettenhofer, by whom I likewise sent the pianoforte arrangement of an *andante* in one of my new symphonies. Nor have I any answer either about the symphony in E flat, that I wished to get. I can now no longer delay inquiring after your own health, as well as that of your husband, and all your dear fam-ily. Is that odious proverb, "Out of sight, out of mind," to prove true everywhere? Oh no! urgent affairs or the loss of my letter and the sym-phony are, no doubt, the cause of your silence. I feel assured of Herr von Kees's willingness to send the symphony, as he said he would do so in his letter; so it seems we shall both have to deplore a loss, and must trust to Providence. I flatter myself I shall receive a short answer to this. Now, my dear, good, kind lady, what is your piano about? Is a thought of Haydn sometimes recalled by your fair hand? Does my sweet Fräulein Pepi ever sing poor "Ariadne?" Oh yes! I seem to hear it even here, especially during the last two months, when I have been residing in the country, amid lovely scenery, with a banker, whose heart and family resemble the Genzingers, and where I live as in a monastery. God be praised! I am in good health, with the exception of my usual rheumatic state. I work hard, and in the early mornings, when I walk in the wood alone with my English grammar, I think of my Creator, of my family, and of all the friends I have left—and of these you are the most valued of all.

I had hoped, indeed, sooner to have enjoyed the felicity of seeing you again; but my circumstances, in short, fate so wills it that I must remain eight or ten months longer in London. Oh, my dear, good lady, how sweet is some degree of liberty! I had a kind Prince, but was obliged at times to be dependent on base souls. I often sighed for release, and now I have it in some measure. I am quite sensible of this benefit, though my mind is burdened with more work. The consciousness of being no longer a bond-servant sweetens all my toils. But, dear as liberty is to me, I do hope on my return again to enter the service of Prince Esterhazy, solely for the sake of my poor family. I doubt much whether I shall find this desire realised, for in his letter my Prince complains of my long absence, and exacts my speedy return in the most absolute terms; which, however, I cannot comply with, owing to a new contract I have entered into here. I, alas! expect my dismissal; but I hope even in that case that God will be gracious to me, and enable me in some degree to remedy the loss by my own industry. Meanwhile I console myself by the hope of soon hearing from you. You shall receive my promised new symphony two months hence; but in order to inspire me with good ideas, I beg you will write to me, and a long letter too.—Yours, etc.

HAYDN.

To Frau v. Gensinger.

LONDON, *Oct.* 13, 1791.

I take the liberty of earnestly entreating you to advance 150 florins for a short time to my wife, provided you do not imagine that since my journey I have become a bad manager. No, my kind, good friend, God blesses my efforts. Three circumstances are alone to blame. In the first place, since I have been here, I have repaid my Prince the 450 florins he advanced for my journey; secondly, I can demand no interest from my bank obligations, having placed them under your care, and not being able to remember either the names or the numbers, so I cannot write a receipt; thirdly, I cannot yet apply for the 5883 florins (1000 of which I recently placed in my Prince's hands, and the rest with the Count v. Fries), especially because it is English money. You will, therefore, see that I am no spendthrift. This leads me to hope that you will not refuse my present request, to lend my wife 150 florins. This letter must be your security, and would be valid in any court. I will repay the interest of the money with a thousand thanks on my return.—I am, etc.,

HAYDN.

. . . I believe you received my letter the very same day that I was reading your cruel reproach that Haydn was capable of forgetting his friend and benefactress. Oh! how often do I long to be beside you at the piano, even for a quarter of an hour, and then to have some good German soup. But we cannot have everything in this world. May God only vouchsafe to grant me the health that I have hitherto enjoyed, and may I preserve it by good conduct and out of gratitude to the Almighty! That you are well is to me the most delightful of all news. May Providence long watch over you! I hope to see you in the course of six months, when I shall, indeed, have much to tell you. Good-night! it is time to go to bed; it is half-past eleven o'clock. One thing more. To insure the safety of the money, Herr Hamberger, a good friend of mine, a man of tall stature, our landlord, will bring you this letter himself, and you can with impunity entrust him with the money; but I beg you will take a receipt both from him and from my wife.

Among other things, Herr v. Kees writes to me that he should like to know my position in London, as there are so many different reports about me in Vienna. From my youth upwards I have been exposed to envy, so it does not surprise me when any attempt is made wholly to crush my poor talents; but the Almighty above is my support. My wife wrote to me that Mozart depreciates me very much, but this I will never believe. If true, I forgive him. There is no doubt that I find many who are envious of me in London also, and I know them almost all. Most of them are Italians. But they can do me no harm, for my credit with this nation has been firmly established far too many years. Rest assured that, if I had not met with a kind reception, I would long since have g-one back to Vienna. I am beloved and esteemed by everyone, except, indeed, professors [of music]. As for my remuneration, Mozart can apply to Count Fries for information, in whose hands I placed 500, and 1000 guilders in those of my Prince, making together nearly 6000 florins. I daily thank my Creator for this boon, and I have good hope that I may bring home a couple of thousands besides, notwithstanding my great outlay and the cost of the journey. I will now no longer intrude on your time. How badly this is written! What is Pater —— doing? My compliments to him.—Yours, etc.   HAYDN.

To Frau v. Genzinger.

LONDON, *Nov.* 17, 1791.

I write in the greatest haste, to request that you will send the accompanying packet, addressed to you, to Herr v. Kees, as it contains the two new symphonies I promised. I waited for a good opportunity, but could hear of none; I have therefore been obliged to send them after all by post. I beg you will ask Herr v. Kees to have a rehearsal of both these symphonies, as they are very delicate, particularly the last movement in D, which I recommend to be given as *pianissimo* as possible, and the *tempo* very quick. I will write to you again in a few days. *Nota bene,* I was obliged to enclose both the symphonies to you, not knowing the address of Herr v. Kees.—I am, etc.

HAYDN.

P. S.—I only returned here to-day from the country. I have been staying with a *mylord* for the last fortnight, a hundred miles from London.

To Frau v. Genzinger.

LONDON, *Dec.* 20, 1791.

I am much surprised that you did not get my letter at the same time as the two symphonies, having put them myself into the post here, and given every direction about them. My mistake was not having enclosed the letter in the packet. This is what often happens, dear lady, with those who have too much head work. I trust, however, that the letter reached you soon afterwards, but in case it did not, I must here explain that both symphonies were intended for Herr v. Kees, but with the stipulation that, after being copied by his order, the scores were to be given up to you, so that you may prepare a pianoforte arrangement of them, if you are so disposed. The particular symphony intended for you will be finished by the end of February at latest. I regret much having been obliged to forward the heavy packet to you, from not knowing Herr v. Kees's address; but he will, of course, repay you the cost of postage, and also, I hope, hand you over seven ducats. May I, therefore, ask you to employ a portion of that sum in copying on small paper my often-applied-for symphony in E minor, and forward it to me by post as soon as possible, for it may perhaps be six months before a courier is despatched from Vienna, and I am in urgent need of the symphony. Further, I must plague you once more by asking you to buy at Artaria's my last pianoforte sonata in

A flat, that is, with 4 B flat minor, with violin and violoncello, and also another piece, the fantasia in C, without accompaniment, for these pieces are not yet published in London; but be so good as not to mention this to Herr Artaria, or he might anticipate the sale in England. I beg you will deduct the price from the seven ducats. To return to the aforesaid symphonies, I must tell you that I sent you a pianoforte arrangement of the *andante* in C minor by Herr Dietten-hofer. It is reported here, however, that he either died on the journey, or met with some serious accident. You had better look over both pieces at your leisure. The principal part of the letter I entrusted to Herr Diettenhofer was the description of a Doctor's degree being conferred on me at Oxford, and all the honours I then received. I must take this opportunity of mentioning that three weeks ago the Prince of Wales invited me to his brother's country seat. The Prince presented me to the Duchess (a daughter of the King of Prussia), who received me very graciously, and said many flattering things. She is the most charming lady in the world, possesses much intelligence, plays the piano, and sings very pleasingly. I stayed two days there, because on the first day a slight indisposition prevented her having any music; on the second day, however, she remained beside me from ten o'clock at night, when the music began, till two hours after midnight. No compositions played but Haydn's. I directed the symphonies at the piano. The sweet little lady sat close beside me at my left hand, and hummed all the pieces from memory, having heard them so repeatedly in Berlin. The Prince of Wales sat on my right hand, and accompanied me very tolerably on the violoncello. They made me sing too. The Prince of Wales is having me painted just now, and the portrait is to be hung up in his private sitting-room. The Prince of Wales is the handsomest man on God's earth; he has an extraordinary love of music, and a great deal of feeling, but very little money. *Nota bene,* this is *entre nous.* His kindness gratifies me far more than any self-interest; on the third day, as I could not get any post-horses, the Duke of York sent me two stages with his own.

Now, dear lady, I should like to reproach you a little for believing that I prefer London to Vienna, and find my residence here more agreeable than in my fatherland. I am far from hating London, but I could not reconcile myself to spend my life there; no, not even to amass millions; my reasons I will tell you when we meet. I think of my home, and embracing once more all my old friends, with the delight of a child; only I deeply lament that the great Mozart will not be of the number, if it be true, which I trust it is not, that he is dead. Posterity will not see such talent as his for the next hundred years! I am happy to hear that you and yours are all so well. I, too, have hitherto been in excellent health, till eight days since, when I was attacked by English rheumatism, and so severely that sometimes I could not help crying out aloud; but I hope soon to get quit of it, as I have adopted the usual custom here, and have wrapped myself up from head to foot in flannel. Pray excuse my bad writing. In the hope of soon being gratified by a letter, and with all esteem for yourself, and best regards to your husband, my dear Fräulein Pepi, and the others—I am, etc.,

HAYDN.

P.S.—Pray give my respects to Herr v. Kreybich [chamber music director to Joseph II].

To Frau v. Genzinger.

LONDON, *Jan.* 17, 1792.

DEAREST AND KINDEST LADY—I must ask your forgiveness a thousand times; and I own and bemoan that I have been too dilatory in the performance of my promise, but if you could only see how I am importuned to attend private concerts, causing me great loss of time, and the mass of work with which I am burdened, you would indeed, dear lady, feel the utmost compassion for me. Never in my life did I write so much in one year as during the last, which has indeed utterly exhausted me, and it wilt do me good to be able to take a little rest when I return home. At present I am working for Salomon's concerts, and feel bound to take all possible trouble, for our rivals of the Professional Society have sent for my pupil Pleyel from Strassburg, to direct their concerts. So a bloody harmonious war will now commence between master and scholar. All the newspapers have begun to discuss the subject, but I think an alliance will soon ensue, my reputation here being so firmly established. Pleyel, on his arrival, displayed so much modesty towards me that he gained my goodwill afresh. We are very often together, which is much to his credit, and he knows how to appreciate his "father;" we will share our laurels fairly, and each go home satisfied. Professional Concerts met with a great misfortune on the 14th of this month, by the Pantheon being entirely burned down, a theatre only built last year. It was the work of an incendiary, and the damage is estimated at more than £100,000 sterling; so there is not a single Italian theatre in London at this moment. Now, my dear angelic lady, I have a little fault to find with you. How often have I reiterated my request to have my symphony in E minor, of which I sent you the theme, copied out on small paper, and sent to me by post? Long have I sighed for it, and if I do not get it by the end of next month I shall lose twenty guineas. Herr v. Kees writes that the copy may possibly arrive in London three months hence, or three years, for there is no chance of a courier being sent off at present. I also told Herr v. Kees in the same letter to take charge of this, and if he could not do so, I ventured to transfer the commission to you flattering myself that my urgent request would, certainly be fulfilled by your kindness. I also desired Herr v. Kees to repay you the cost of the postage you paid for his packet. Kindest and most charming Frau v. Genzinger, I once more beg you to see to this matter, for it is really a work of mercy, and when we meet I will explain my reasons, respectfully kiss your fair hands, and repay my debt with gratitude. The celebration you mention in honour of my poor abilities touched me deeply, but still not so profoundly as if you had considered it more perfect. Perhaps I may supply this imperfection by another symphony which I will shortly send you; I say *perhaps,* because I (or rather my brain) am in truth weary. Providence alone can repair the deficiency in my powers, and to Him I daily pray for aid, for without His support I should indeed be a poor creature! And now, my kind and dear friend, I venture to hope for your indulgence. Oh yes! your portrait is at this moment before me, and I hear it say, "Well, for this time, you odious Haydn, I will forgive you, but—but!" No, no, I mean henceforth strictly to fulfil my duties. I must conclude for to-day by saying that now, as ever, I am, with the highest esteem, yours, etc.,

HAYDN.

To Frau v. Genzinger.

LONDON, *Feb.* 2, 1792.

I have today received your kind letter, and also the fantasia, and sonata *a tre.* I was, however, rather vexed, on opening the packet, not to find the long-looked-for symphony in E minor, which I had fully hoped for, and expected. Dear lady, I entreat you to send it at once, written on small post paper, and I will gladly pay all expenses, for Heaven alone can tell when the symphonies from Brussels may arrive here. I cannot dispense with this one, without incurring great loss. Pray forgive my plaguing you so often on the subject, but I shall indeed be truly grateful if you will send it. Being overwhelmed with work at present, I cannot as yet write to Herr v. Kees. Pray, then, apply to him yourself for the said symphony. With my kind respects, I am, yours, etc.,

HAYDN.

You shall have a good portion of the sewing needles.

To Frau v. Genzinger.

LONDON, *March 2,* 1792.

Yesterday morning I received your valued letter, and also the long-looked-for symphony. I humbly kiss your hands for sending it so safely and quickly. I had indeed received it six days previously from Brussels, through Herr v. Kees; but the score was more useful, as a good deal must be altered in it to suit the English taste. I only regret that I must trouble you so frequently with my commissions, especially as at present I cannot adequately testify my gratitude. I do positively assure and declare to you that this causes me great embarrassment, and indeed often makes me feel very sad; the more so that, owing to various urgent causes, I am unable to send you as yet the new symphony dedicated to you. First, because I wish to alter and embellish the last movement, which is too feeble when compared with the first. I felt this conviction myself quite as much as the public, when it was performed for the first time last Friday; notwithstanding which, it made the most profound impression on the audience. The second reason is that I really dread the risk of its falling into other hands. I was not a little startled when I read the unpleasant intelligence about the sonata. By Heavens! I would rather have lost twenty-five ducats than have suffered such a theft, and the only one who can have done this is my own copyist; but I fervently hope to supply the loss through Madame Tost, for I do not wish to incur any reproaches from her. You must therefore, dear lady, be indulgent towards me, until I can towards the end of July myself have the pleasure of placing in your hands the sonata, as well as the symphony. *Nota bene,* the symphony is to be given by myself, but the sonata by Madame Tost. It is equally impossible for me to send Herr v. Kees the promised symphonies at present, for here too there is a great want of faithful copyists. If I had time, I would write them out myself, but no day, not a single one, am I free from work, and I shall thank the good Lord when I can leave London; the sooner the better. My labours are augmented by the arrival of my pupil Pleyel, who has been summoned here by the Professional Society to direct their concerts.

He brought with him a number of new compositions, which were, however, written long ago! He accordingly promised to give a new piece every evening. On seeing this, I could easily perceive that there was a dead set against me, so I also announced publicly that I would likewise give twelve different new pieces; so in order to keep my promise, and to support poor Salomon, I must be the victim, and work perpetually. I do feel it, however, very much. My eyes suffer most, and my nights are very sleepless, but with God's help I will overcome it all. The Professors wished to put a spoke in my wheel because I did not join their concerts, but the public is just. Last year I received great applause, but this year still more. Pleyel's presumption is everywhere criticised, and yet I love him, and have gone to his concert each time, and been the first to applaud him. I sincerely rejoice that you and yours are well. My kind regards to all. The time draws near to put my trunks in travelling order. Oh! how delighted shall I be to see you again, and to show personally all the esteem that I felt for you in absence, and that I ever shall feel for you.—Yours, etc.,

HAYDN.

P.S.—Please apologise to Herr v. Kees for want of time preventing my sending him the new symphonies. I hope to have the honour of directing them myself in your house, at our next Christmas music.

To Frau v. Genzinger.

LONDON, *April* 24, 1792.

I yesterday evening received with much pleasure your last letter of 5 April, with the extract from the newspaper, extolling my poor talents to the Viennese. I must confess that I have gained considerable credit with the English in vocal music, by this little chorus,[33] my first attempt with English words. It is only to be regretted that, during my stay here, I have not been able to write more pieces of a similar nature, but we could not find any boys to sing at our concerts, they having been already engaged for a year past to sing at other concerts, of which there are a vast number. In spite of the great opposition of my musical enemies, who are so bitter against me, more especially leaving nothing undone with my pupil Pleyel this winter to humble me, still, thank God! I may say that I have kept the upper hand. I must, however, admit that I am quite wearied and worn out with so much work, and look forward with eager longing to the repose which will soon take pity on me. I thank you, dear lady, for your kind solicitude about me. Just as you thought, I do not require to go to Paris at present, from a variety of reasons, which I will tell you when we meet. I am in daily expectation of an order from my Prince, to whom I wrote lately, to tell me where I am to go. It is possible that he may summon me to Frankfort; if not, I intend (*entre nous*) to go by Holland to the King of Prussia at Berlin, thence to Leipzig, Dresden, Prague, and last of all to Vienna, where I hope to embrace all my friends.—Ever, with high esteem, etc.,

HAYDN.

Notes

[1] See an interesting account of a visit to the cottage after the fire, in *The Musical Times* for July 1899.

[2] See Miss Townsend's *Haydn*, p.9.

[3] The relations of Haydn and Porpora are sketched in George Sand's *Consuelo*.

[4] Miss Townsend's *Haydn*, p.44.

[5] See an interesting account of "Il Ritorno di Tobia" in *The Musical Times* for September 1901, p.600.

[6] See *Letters of Distinguished Musicians*. Translated from the German by Lady Wallace. London, 1867.

[7] See *Musical Haunts in London*, by F.G. Edwards, London, 1895.

[8] See *Musical Haunts in London*, F. G. Edwards, quoting Dr. W. H. Cummings.

[9] See the Appendix to Shield's *Introduction to Harmony*.

[10] This might be effected by the violin player having the drumstick tied to his right foot, which was sometimes done.

[11] Jones was organist of St. Paul's Cathedral at this time. His chant, which was really in the key of D, has since been supplanted. Haydn made an error in bar 12.

[12] See Berlioz's *Life and Letters*, English edition, Vol. I., p.281.

[13] The portrait, a whole length, was sold in 1798 for £325.,10s., and again at Christie's, in 1845, for 505 guineas—to an American, as usual.

[14] The scandalous Jacobin persecutions and executions in Austria and Hungary took place in 1796.

[15] See note by C. H. Purday in *Leisure Hour* for 1880, p.528.

[16] In one of George Thomson's letters to Mrs Hunter we read: "It is not the first time that your muse and Haydn's have met, as we see from the beautiful canzonets. Would he had been directed by you about the words to 'The Creation!' It is lamentable to see such divine music joined with such miserable broken English. He (Haydn) wrote me lately that in three years, by the performance of 'The Creation' and 'The Seasons' at Vienna, 40,000 florins had been raised for the poor families of musicians."

[17] See J. F. Runciman's *Old Scores and New Readings*, where an admirably just and concise appreciation of Haydn and "The Creation" may be read.

[18] Fled forever is my strength; old and weak am I.

[19] The letters passed through the present writer's hands some five years ago, when he was preparing his *Life of George Thompson* (1898). They are now in the British Museum with the other Thompson correspondence.

[20] The great masters have been peculiarly unfortunate in the matter of their "remains." When Beethoven's grave was opened in 1863, Professor Wagner

was actually allowed to cut off the ears and aural cavities of the corpse in order to investigate the cause of the dead man's deafness. The alleged skeleton of Sebastian Bach was taken to an anatomical museum a few years ago, "cleaned up," and clothed with a semblance of flesh to show how Bach looked in life! Donizetti's skull was stolen before the funeral, and was afterwards sold to a pork butcher, who used it as a money-bowl. Gluck was re-buried in 1890 beside Mozart, Beethoven and Schubert, after having lain in the little suburban churchyard of Matzleinsdorf since 1787.

[21] See *Records of My Life*, by John Taylor: London, 1832.

[22] "His notes had such little heads and slender tails that he used, very properly, to call them his *flies' legs*."—*Bombet*, p.97.

[23] Compare Mozart's words as addressed to Michael Kelly: "Melody is the essence of music. I should liken one who invents melodies to a noble racehorse, and a mere contrapuntist to a hired post-hack."

[24] See *Studies of Great Composers,* by C. Hubert H. Parry, p.109.

[25] Compare Professor Prout's *Treatise on Harmony.*

[26] See W.J. Hendersons' *How Music Developed*, p.191: London, 1899.

[27] See Ernst Pauer's *Musical Forms.*

[28] See *The Pianoforte Sonata,* by J. S. Shedlock: London, 1895. Mr Shedlock, by selecting for analysis some of the most characteristic sonatas, shows Haydn in his three stages of apprenticeship, mastery and maturity.

[29] Compare *The Orchestra and Orchestral Music,* by W. J. Henderson: London, 1901.

[30] The portion of the letter deleted is that given at page 161, beginning, "I lost twenty pounds in weight."

[31] Joseph A., one of the Genzinger children.

[32] Franz, author of the Genzinger children.

[33] The " Storm Chorus," *see* p. 56.

Index